The Last Photograph

A Novel By

Anne Miller

To my parents, Howard and Geraldine Miller:
You gave me the greatest gift as a child: a typewriter and an endless supply of blank paper to let my imagination run wild on. You were afraid I threw it all away when I left college, but I think it's safe to say now that I just took the scenic route. Love you always.

Acknowledgments

I would like to thank first and foremost God for blessing me with this amazing gift of writing, and for giving me the strength and perseverance to see this dream through to reality.

To my good friend Lisa Masanova for being my biggest cheerleader on this journey. It's taken a long time, but you've been with me every step of the way, always encouraging me to never give up; constantly reminding me that I do have what it takes, and my words are worthy to be shared with the rest of the world. For that I will be eternally grateful to you.

To my family: never once did any of you ever tell me I couldn't, or shouldn't, keep chasing my dream of becoming a published author, and that means the world to me. A special thank you goes out to my sister Donna for being my Jane Q Reader. You listened to me recite sentences over and over again and willingly gave your opinion as to which word sounded better. Now we'll see if you were right or not.

To everyone who took the time to answer all the questions I asked to make this story more authentic: Davin Lindwall, Dave at Cutting

Edge Photography, and Joe Bortolameoli for the motorcycle insight. It's been a while since I asked, but I still remember and appreciate all your help.

To the Upper Peninsula Publishers and Authors Association for introducing me to Tyler Tichelaar who became my editor, and Larry Alexander who became my layout designer. Thank you both so much for all your help and generosity and for being so patient with me throughout this entire process. This was definitely an eye-opening experience for me, and I don't know how I would have ever done this without you guys.

A big thank you to Tara, Kenzie, and last but not least, Laura at CJ Graphics. Your opinions, passionate enthusiasm, and artistic talent all came together to make this gorgeous cover art that is cooler than anything I could have ever imagined.

To all the authors I have met along the way—Jim Jackson, Sally Beauchamp, Doc Stupp, just to name a few—thank you for taking the time to talk to and listen to me. Writing can sometimes be a very solitary career path. It's comforting to know I am not the only one, especially in the UP, taking the road less traveled.

And finally, to all my friends who have been eagerly awaiting the publication of this book. Here's hoping the rest of the world will be just as excited to get their hands on it as you all are.

Chapter One

This was the perfect opportunity—the magic hour—but Adrian Cattrel had to play it just right. If she moved too suddenly or made too much noise, he might wake up and then it would all be over.

She lay motionless on her side while her mind raced. Her eyes darted from her alarm clock to the light filtering through the long gray blinds. Adrian bit her lip and squeezed her pillow. It wouldn't be long now.

She bided her time until Jake's snoring grew loud and intense. She rolled over and inched upward.

Adrian peeked at him. So far so good; he was still out like a light. She let out a soft sigh of relief before she continued.

Adrian reached cautiously for her camera—a DSLR Nikon D7000 she had received as a gift—which she kept in the drawer of her nightstand specifically for moments like this.

This was what she liked to call a living moment—one that wasn't planned or posed for; it just happened, and living moments were her absolute favorite to photograph. Her closet overflowed with photo albums full of all different kinds of them, but none meant more to her than this one because Jake had eluded her for so long.

Adrian could never catch him off guard like this. Somehow, Jake always knew when she had her camera pointed at him, and as she would press the button, he'd roll the other way or sit up and make a face at her—whatever it took to ruin the moment. But not this morning.

Her eyes were drawn to their wedding picture that stood atop her nightstand. She kept it in a silver frame, positioned so that it was the first thing she saw when she woke up in the morning. Corny, Adrian knew, but acceptable seeing as how they had just celebrated their one-year anniversary last weekend.

The photograph was of their first dance together as a married couple. She had her arms wrapped around his neck while he dipped her backwards. Neither one seemed to realize their picture was even being taken—Adrian caught in her own living moment.

A goofy grin spread uncontrollably across her face.

All right now, that's enough! We need to focus here. Concentrate!

Adrian leaned farther back against the headboard while she switched to her 85mm lens. She winced every time she made the slightest sound, fearful it might jolt him awake.

But it didn't.

Adrian snuck anxiously out of bed. She raised the camera up to her eye, then paused to take him in.

Jake lay on his back. He had his right arm flung across the pillow; his head nestled on his arm; his long blonde bangs fell haphazardly into his eyes. She wanted to brush them away so badly, but she craved the picture even more, so she settled down and took a few quick test shots instead.

Adrian snapped the shutter button incessantly while she tiptoed across the room. She stopped in front of the window. The sun hung low in the early morning sky, but one golden ray still managed to capture her husband's serene face in its glow.

Husband. Adrian smiled again. If anybody would've ever told her after their first meeting that she'd end up marrying Jake Riley, she would've asked them what kind of drugs they were on.

*

It all began the summer before Adrian's senior year of college at the University of Wisconsin–Green Bay. She and her best friend, Cassie Adler, decided to stick around instead of returning home during the break. They found a cheap but decent apartment downtown to rent, along with landing the perfect summer jobs as lifeguards at the Humboldt Park community pool. In fact, the park was exactly where Adrian was coming from on that hot, humid, summer afternoon.

It had been a particularly grueling shift—a test in patience that Adrian had failed miserably. She normally loved being around kids, but not today. These kids knew just how to push her buttons, and once they figured it out, they wouldn't quit. All Adrian wanted to do now was get home and take a nice cold shower, but she sat slumped behind the steering wheel of her silver Saturn instead.

Adrian cursed while she raised her arm in a futile attempt to wipe the sweat from her brow. She should have gotten the air conditioning fixed as soon as it died on her, but she thought she could live without it. She had never expected to be stuck in bumper-to-bumper traffic on Mason Street during one of the hottest days on record. Although she did have to admit, she could've avoided all of this if she would've just listened.

The local media had been warning drivers for weeks about the major road construction that was going to take place downtown throughout the summer. Cassie had even mapped out an alternate route for her to take to and from work. But Adrian had stuffed that map inside her glove compartment along with all her debit card receipts, straw wrappers, and napkins from all of the fast food places she frequented.

After twenty minutes of sitting among other trapped, idling vehicles, Adrian plugged in her iPod and cranked up the volume in the hopes of simmering her rapidly boiling temper. She tapped her hand against the steering wheel in time to "Barracuda," but by the time "American Woman" came on, her tapping had turned into nothing more than pounding on the wheel in frustration.

This was worse than being on Lombardi Avenue right after a Packer game let out. She glanced down at her watch and groaned. The only thing that seemed to be moving ahead was the time. She grimaced as a bead of sweat trickled down her back. Adrian craned her neck out the window. All she saw ahead of her were more frustrated drivers, screaming and honking their horns like mad.

What the hell are they doing up there? Repaving the fucking road by hand?

Just when Adrian thought she was going to melt right onto the driver's seat, something amazing happened. She thought it was a mirage at first, but she blinked her eyes and realized that, yes indeed, the vehicles in front of her were actually moving forward!

"Thank you, God!"

The words no sooner left her mouth than the sign man—some young, bodybuilder type who seemed more concerned about texting than his actual job—suddenly flipped the sign around from "'slow" to "stop." Adrian slammed on her brakes, stuck in neutral once again.

The sign man noticed her the second she screeched to a halt in front of him. He slowly lowered his black Ray-Bans to get a better look at her. She fell instantaneously under the spell his bright, baby-blue eyes cast upon her.

Adrian had never seen anything like them before. They had to be contacts. No way that was a natural eye color.

The spell was broken seconds later when she caught those same gorgeous eyes inspecting every inch of her as if she were a choice piece of meat in a butcher shop. But the thing that really pushed her over the edge was his smug smile of satisfaction.

Her almond-colored eyes blazed. She could take no more today. This guy had gone too far.

"And just what the hell are you looking at?" she hissed while she leaned out the window.

"Whoa," he said, his palms up. "Take it easy there, sweet thing. I was just admiring the view."

"First off, I am not your sweet thing, and secondly—"

"Hey, lady," the guy in the SUV behind her suddenly screamed. "Stick your head back in your car and move it already."

"Read the sign, asshole," said Adrian, pointing her finger emphatically at the sign. "It says—"

"Slow!" the driver yelled.

Adrian did a double-take after she actually looked at the sign herself. It had changed from "stop" to "slow." The sign man flashed her a wicked smile as she slunk back into her seat.

"Bye-bye, sweet thing," he said as he waved to Adrian.

Adrian responded by flipping him off before she got back into her car. She wanted to spin her wheels and spray gravel at him, but she decided the fine she'd have to pay wouldn't be worth it.

*

Adrian stormed into her apartment later that afternoon with all the rage of a full-blown hurricane. She threw her duffel bag onto the floor and slammed the front door shut as hard as she could. Cassie shot up from the couch like a jack-in-the-box and stared fearfully at her friend. A box fan whirred on full blast beside her while Blake Shelton blared from her laptop.

"Can you please turn that shit off?" Adrian asked with what little restraint she had left.

"Okay, okay," Cassie obliged while she killed the music. "Jesus. What's your problem?"

"My problem? Well, let's see…it could be the fact that I was surrounded by the Children of the Corn all day today, or it might have something to do with the damn construction I got trapped in on my way home," Adrian fumed as she stomped into the living room.

"Construction? What construction? You shouldn't have had to go through any construction." Cassie slowly folded her arms while she waited for Adrian to answer her. Adrian avoided her friend's interrogating eyes. "You didn't take Taylor to Ninth like I told you to, did you?"

"Well…no," Adrian mumbled.

"So that's why you're in such a glorious mood."

"That, and there was a major asshole working on the road crew."

"Wait a minute. Back up the bus there, missy," Cassie interrupted. "There's a guy involved too?"

"Mmm-hmm," Adrian grumbled.

"Well, this is going to be a much more interesting story than I thought. I'm going to have to get comfortable now." Cassie sank back into her pink camouflage pillow and stretched out her long legs. "All right, continue."

Adrian laughed despite herself. She grabbed the fan and turned it toward her before she sat down on the other end of the couch and vented to her best friend.

"Well," Cassie said after Adrian had finished, "it sounds to me like someone needs to take a trip to The Borderline."

Most women turn to comfort food like a pint of mint chocolate chip ice cream or a package of Double Stuf Oreos whenever they get depressed or upset, but not Cassie and Adrian. They had a comfort bar.

Adrian and Cassie sauntered through the front door of The Borderline an hour later. The scent of deep-fried food filled Adrian's nostrils; peanut shells crunched underneath her feet, and the drum solo from Phil Collins' "In The Air Tonight" pounded in her ears.

Ah, home sweet home, Adrian thought.

"Hey, there's my girls!"

A petite, slender woman in her mid-fifties with long, honey-blonde hair leapt from her barstool and wrapped her tattooed arms around Adrian and Cassie.

"Hey, Maggie!" they greeted their favorite bartender in unison.

"So, what are you girls up to tonight?"

"Ah, you know," Adrian shrugged. "No better place to beat the heat than here."

"Uh-huh." Maggie crossed her arms while she studied Adrian. "So who is he and what did he do to piss you off?"

"I never said anything about a guy."

"You didn't have to. I've seen that look in your eyes way too many times before."

"We need to get some shots of tequila in this girl ASAP," Cassie said while she slung her arm around Adrian's neck.

"Absolutely," Maggie agreed, "right after we get some food in her."

"Yes, Mom," Adrian teased.

"Hey, watch it now!" Maggie pointed her finger at Adrian. Her eyebrow arched in amusement as she backpedaled toward the kitchen.

The shots and the beer went down way too easily, even after Adrian and Cassie polished off a basket of hot wings and an order of double-decker nachos. The girls' barstool danced to Jimmy Buffet and Alan Jackson, who were proclaiming it was five o'clock somewhere on the jukebox, and Maggie had them laughing so hard at her best male-bashing jokes that they didn't even notice the group of men who ambled in behind them.

The majority of them looked to be interested in finding the quickest route to the coldest beer, but Jake Riley detoured away from the rest, a move that didn't go unnoticed by his best friend Charlie Winslow.

"Jake, you're heading the wrong way brother! You're never gonna get a drink over there!"

Jake replied with an impatient wave of his hand while he continued on toward the more crowded section of the bar. Charlie kept his eyes on him until he saw the two girls Jake had set his sights on.

"Then again," Charlie laughed to himself, "maybe a drink's not what you're after."

"Uh, oh," Adrian said as she raised her bottle up close to her face. "I'm almost empty."

"Huh," Cassie replied while she shook hers. "Look at that. Mine's already gone."

"Hey, Maggie!" Adrian leaned over to get her attention and nearly hit her head on one of the many piñatas that hung above the bar. "We need another round down here, pronto!"

Maggie glanced down at them before she turned to her longtime boyfriend, Tony, who sat beside her.

"Well," Maggie asked him, "what do you think? Do we need to cut them off yet?"

Adrian and Cassie fluttered their eyelashes at him. Tony laughed.

"Naw," he answered, his voice deep and raspy from smoking too many cigarettes over the years, "I think they're still good."

The girls blew kisses at him in thanks.

Maggie brought them their beers. Adrian leaned back on her stool and stared expectantly at Cassie.

"What?" Cassie asked.

"It's your turn," Adrian answered.

"Oh, no," Cassie protested. "I paid for the last round."

"No, I did."

"Adrian."

"Cassie."

"Ladies, please; allow me."

They stopped arguing once they saw a tan, muscular arm stretched out between them to place a twenty-dollar bill on the bar. Both women looked over their shoulders to see whom they needed to thank for his generosity.

Cassie flipped her fingers through her short blonde hair and flashed him her best flirtatious smile. Adrian rolled her eyes and groaned in disgust.

"You've got to be kidding me," Adrian said.

"Hey there, sweet thing," he said as his lips broadened into a devilish smile. "Long time no see."

Adrian's blood began to boil all over again.

"I'm not thirsty anymore," she said coolly.

"Adrian," Cassie scolded her.

"I need to go play some good music," Adrian fumed as if she hadn't even heard her friend. "That's enough of this country shit."

"Adrian, wait."

Cassie chased her to the jukebox. Adrian flipped absently back and forth through the list of songs she practically knew by heart until Cassie couldn't take it anymore. She slammed the palm of her hand down on the glass. Adrian stared at her in shock.

"What the hell?" Adrian asked.

"Yeah, 'what the hell' is right," Cassie snapped. "A hot guy offers to buy us a round of drinks and you bail on him? What, did the heat melt your brain out there today or something?"

"No. It's just that your hot guy over there is my asshole from this afternoon."

"What?" Cassie shrieked as she glanced over her shoulder. "No way!"

"Mm-hm," Adrian replied indifferently.

"But he's so hot!"

Adrian shot her a dirty look. "Really?"

"Sorry. My hormones overtook my brain there for a second, but I'm back now. But seriously, you should be making him buy all your drinks for you tonight."

"I don't think so."

"Why not? He owes you that much, especially after the way he treated you today."

Adrian chewed on her lip while she stared uncertainly at her friend.

"You know, you do make a good point."

"Don't I always?" Cassie asked with a lopsided grin. "C'mon, Aide; what are you waiting for?"

"Fine," Adrian sighed. "You talked me into it."

"Good girl."

They finished making their picks on the jukebox and were on their way back to the bar when Adrian felt someone's hand on her shoulder. She turned around to see Tony glaring down at her.

"Hey, Tony," she tried to yell above the noise of the crowd. "How goes it?"

He leaned down to whisper in her ear. "That guy at the bar before. He giving you any trouble?"

Adrian put a reassuring hand on Tony's arm. "It's okay. I got it all under control."

Tony narrowed his eyes and stared skeptically at her. "Uh, huh. Well, if you need me, you know where to find me."

"Thanks, Tony."

"Anytime, hon."

He gave her shoulder a gentle squeeze before he blended back into the crowd.

"Sorry," Adrian apologized once she reached Cassie. "I had to convince Tony not to try out one of his new bouncer moves on the sign guy."

"Well," Cassie paused while she took a drink of her beer, "you might want to rethink that."

"What? Why?"

Cassie jutted her chin out in front of her. Adrian followed her friend's gaze down the length of the bar where she saw the sign guy standing underneath a brightly-colored donkey piñata. Skinny women in tight blue jeans and form-fitting tank tops that barely contained their breasts surrounded him. Two of them hung all over him. His face lit up like a Christmas tree. Adrian shook her head and scoffed.

"Jackass," she said.

He caught her watching him. Adrian whipped around toward Cassie, but it was too late. The next thing she knew, she felt him hovering over her.

"You came back," he said.

"And you left." Adrian turned to face him. "Big surprise there."

"Oh, c'mon; don't be like that now. You're making me feel bad."

"Good. You should."

"All right," he said with a slight nod. "I'll admit, I deserved that. So now why don't you let me make it up to you by buying you a drink?"

Adrian put her hand on her hip, cocked her head to the side, and stared at him in disbelief. She was just about to say something when one of the women from his posse stumbled over.

"There you are, Jakie!" Her voice sounded as high and shrill as fingernails on a chalkboard. She threw her arms around him as if she had known him forever. Adrian leaned back to avoid having half the woman's mixed drink land in her lap. "C'mon; we can't do another round of Jell-O shots without you!"

Adrian rolled her eyes while Jake's dropped to the floor. Her back was to him again within a matter of seconds.

"You know what, Candy?" Jake told the woman while he gently unraveled her arms. "I think I'm all shot out for tonight."

"Well, you don't have to drink one. You could just watch us."

"Oh, good God," Adrian muttered under her breath.

Just then, a young black man sidled up to Candy from out of nowhere.

"Sweetheart, I'd be more than happy to do as many shots with you as you would like tonight."

Candy blinked in confusion before she turned to Jake, who gave her an encouraging grin.

Ah, Adrian thought, *must be his wingman.*

"Awesome!" Candy replied as she accepted Charlie's outstretched arm.

Adrian waited until she heard Candy's stiletto heels click away before she spoke again.

"What are you doing?" she asked Jake sarcastically. "You're going to miss out on a golden opportunity with Barbie and all of her friends."

Jake smiled as he tipped his bottle of beer to his lips. "That's Charlie's golden opportunity, not mine. Besides," he added as he turned to her and held her captive with his eyes, "there is nowhere else I would rather be right now."

It wasn't just what he said but how he said it that made Adrian melt. Maggie stood before them behind the bar mixing drinks, and even she couldn't help swooning over Jake's words. They both stared at her until she made a quick exit with a fake cough.

"Look, I'm sure that line's worked wonders for you before with other women—"

"It's not a line." He raised his right hand. "I swear to God."

"Yeah, right. Like you'd even tell me if it was."

"Well no," he admitted with a self-deprecating smile, "probably not. But if I were just looking for someone to sleep with, don't you think I'd still be with Barbie and all of her friends?"

If this had been any other guy, Adrian would've made some smartass comeback and walked away. But there was something about Jake— something she couldn't quite pinpoint or explain. He wasn't just any other guy, and Adrian didn't want to let this moment end just yet.

"Go on," she replied.

"So what do you think?" he asked her. "Have I earned the right to buy you that drink now?"

Adrian responded by pushing her beer bottle forward to the edge of the bar.

*

A low, guttural growl escaped from deep inside Jake's dreams. He shifted restlessly from one side to the other before finally settling onto his back. The blanket and sheets were all crumpled together at the end of the bed. His head angled down toward her as if he were trying to avoid the light. Jake's mouth hung wide open; his right arm bent across his smooth, bare chest as if he were imitating Celine Dion performing "My Heart Will Go On."

Adrenaline pumped through Adrian's veins as she held the camera up to her eye once more. It was all she could do to keep her hands from shaking like an addict going through withdrawals while she zoomed in on his face.

That's when Adrian heard him mumble something in his sleep.

"Morning, sweet thing," Jake said before his eyes popped open and he stared at her with a mischievous grin on his face.

"Jake!"

Adrian sounded angry with him, but the curve of her lips said otherwise.

Those damn eyes of his!

They were the first thing that had attracted her to him when they had met four years ago, and they still made her go weak in the knees now, even though she looked into them every single day.

She raked her fingers through her long, dark hair, which seemed to have run wilder than usual during the night while she slept.

"Oh, c'mon; you're not really mad at me, are you?"

Adrian didn't say a word, but her pissed off expression began to fade as Jake crept closer to her.

"You can't do it," he teased, his face inches away from hers. "You're trying awfully damn hard, but it's not going to happen."

"You think so, huh?" Adrian asked him.

"Oh, I know so."

And with that, he set her camera carefully back onto the nightstand before he blew softly into her ear.

"Oh…so not fair," she moaned.

"Now who said anything about playing fair, sweet thing?" he whispered.

Adrian shivered. Goosebumps covered her arms while Jake's lips traveled from her ear down the length of her long, slender neck. She scrambled to bring his lips back up to hers, and once she did, their tongues entwined in a kiss so intense that Adrian found herself underneath Jake.

Jake ripped her T-shirt off and flung it onto the floor. He stared voraciously down at his wife before he began his sensual assault on her.

He ran the tip of his finger ever so slowly around one of her nipples before his mouth devoured her breast.

Adrian's mind was already on sensory overload when Jake's fingers wandered further down to give her a more intimate massage, and that's when her desire took control.

She flipped Jake over onto his back and pinned him down by his wrists.

"Whoa," Jake said, his eyes alive with excitement, "what's gotten into you?"

"Nothing," Adrian smirked, "yet."

She held his wrists over his head with one hand while the other glided down to where she much rather wanted it to be. Her eyes never left his while she stroked the length of him, slowly at first, then faster and with much more intensity.

"Payback's a bitch, isn't it?" Adrian whispered wickedly into her husband's ear before her mouth ventured down to relieve her hand.

A seductive smile spread across her lips moments later as she straddled Jake and guided him assertively inside her.

"You are one dirty girl," Jake said afterwards as they lay blissfully exhausted together.

Adrian laughed.

"You know what that means, don't you?"

"No," she said as she looked up at him. "What?"

"I'm going to have to clean you up now."

It took a moment for her to catch on.

"Oh, no!"

"Oh, yes."

Adrian's eyes widened as he scooped her up and carried her into their bathroom.

"Jake!"

"Shh," he said as his mouth came inches away from her lips. "Just shut up and enjoy the ride, will you."

"Yes, sir," she said, saluting him before she buried her face in his neck and prepared to get very wet.

*

Adrian peeked out from behind the bathroom door after they had finished their shower to see whether Jake was still in the room.

Nope. No sign of him anywhere.

She tiptoed across the room wearing nothing but a bath towel wrapped around her. She headed straight for the closet and pulled out a blue flannel shirt of Jake's.

Adrian loved to wear this shirt around the house, but it drove Jake crazy. He said he could never wear it after she did because it always smelled like a girl. So Adrian came up with a plan to alleviate that problem.

I'll just throw it in the wash before Jake gets home. He'll never suspect a thing.

She had just slid her arms into his shirt and was about to go search for some pants when she noticed the note propped up against her camera:

"Couldn't wait. You made me late. Love ya, sweet thing."

Adrian smiled fondly while she folded up the sheet of paper and tucked it into her shirt pocket. The notes her husband left her were not the makings of legendary Shakespearean sonnets, but it could be worse. At least he could tell her he loved her every once in a while.

Jake never wore his heart on his sleeve. That just wasn't his style, and that had everything to do with the way his dad had raised him.

Kevin Riley wasn't a single father. He and Jake's mother, Laura, were happily married for sixteen years. There must've been many times throughout their marriage, though, Adrian assumed, when Laura felt like a single parent.

Kevin had driven a truck cross country for a living, which meant he wasn't around as much as he would've liked to have been. He did call every night from wherever he was on the road, and he utilized those conversations as well as any other opportunity he had with his only child to instill in him the true meaning of being a real man, according to the generations of Riley men who came before them.

A real man. Adrian scoffed while she slung her camera carefully over her shoulder, tucked her laptop under her arm, and walked down the hallway to the kitchen.

She opened the top cupboard to pull out her favorite economy-sized coffee mug. Then she reached into the refrigerator for the gallon of chocolate milk. Her smile vanished when she noticed that the container was almost empty. Jake never touched it, so she had no one to blame but herself.

Oh, God, how could I have forgotten to get another gallon yesterday?

She cringed while she poured. There wasn't nearly as much as she wanted, but it would have to do.

She wrote "CHOCOLATE MILK!!!" on a Post-it note and stuck it on the front of her purse. Hopefully, that would be enough to remind her to stop at the grocery store on her way home from the photo shoot she was working at. Adrian beamed with pride while she slid the morning paper off the kitchen counter and headed straight for the French doors.

No, she wasn't a professional photographer yet, but she was working for one—Samantha Lancaster to be exact—and that alone was enough to make her pinch herself sometimes to make sure it was really happening.

Adrian stepped out onto the balcony that wrapped around the entire second story of the old rambling Victorian home they rented in downtown Green Bay. She stood there for a moment and basked in the morning sunlight that was already heating up most of Ashland Avenue. She took in a deep breath of summertime air before she sat down in her white wicker chair, stretched out her legs, and began her morning ritual.

Adrian snapped open the newspaper and immediately flipped to the sports page to see how her beloved Cubbies had done the night before. She had been a fan ever since she could remember. It was all her dad's fault. He was originally from Chicago and bound and determined to pass his obsession for Cubs' baseball onto his child. Her head hung low when she saw the score. Another loss, but her team was tough. They'd bounce back. Adrian was sure of it.

Ah, toughness. The essential ingredient needed to become a real man. And just how did a boy get tough? By keeping all his emotions locked up inside of him, holding them all in so he could be strong for everyone else around him.

Adrian shook her head in disbelief while she tossed the paper on the table.

What a line of crap, but Jake bought every single word of it because his father was the one who sold it to him.

Laura had warned Adrian all about this a long time ago back when

Jake had first introduced Adrian to his mother.

Our first meeting. Now that was a trip and a half!

Adrian didn't intimidate easily. She went head-to-head with the captain of her high school football team after he ditched Cassie at the homecoming dance for another girl. So this shouldn't have fazed her at all, but it did.

Adrian couldn't remember a time, as she and Jake walked into Mama Jo's Pizzeria, when she had felt more vulnerable.

Mama Jo's wasn't just any pizza place. It was an institution like Wrigley Field; one that was built upon Josephine Miceli's secret pizza sauce and continued to thrive today through her granddaughter, Laura Riley.

It was close to closing time when Laura asked her son to go into the kitchen to see whether his cousins needed any help cleaning up. Adrian gripped the table a little tighter while she and Laura faced off across the booth from each other.

"So," Laura began, "you're in love with my son."

It wasn't a question. It was a statement, and one that Adrian wasn't prepared for.

Laura chuckled when she saw the blindsided look on Adrian's face.

"I know," Mrs. Riley continued. "It shocked me too."

Adrian stared at her boyfriend's mother in bewilderment.

"Don't get me wrong; I love my son." She paused to sip her wine. "But he's not the easiest man for anyone else to love."

Adrian bit her tongue.

"You know," Laura glanced over her shoulder to make sure Jake wasn't coming back yet, "I haven't seen that boy cry since he was little."

"Seriously?"

"Seriously. The last time he even came close was when his dad was trying to teach him how to ride his bike.

"I'll never forget it. I was watching them from the kitchen window. Jake fell and skinned his knee pretty bad. I just about broke my neck getting to the front door after I saw him hit the ground. My first instinct was to scoop him up in my arms and make sure he was okay, but Kevin stopped me. I saw him lean down and whisper something in Jake's ear that made that boy's tears vanish for good."

"What did he say?"

"Don't know, but I wouldn't be surprised if Kevin quoted something from his Riley Man's Bible to him."

Adrian didn't say a word.

"Oh, c'mon; don't act like you don't know what I'm talking about. You can't tell me you've never seen Jake in his Riley stance before."

The Riley stance was a position Jake stood in: legs spread apart, shoulders back, chest out, head held high whenever he came too close to showing too much emotion. Adrian had experienced it first-hand many times before and it drove her absolutely crazy.

"Oh, yeah," Adrian mumbled while she fiddled with the damp napkin underneath her glass of beer, "I have."

"So you know what you're getting into? I'm only asking because most of the girls my son's introduced me to thought they could change him and, well, you can see how far that got them."

"I'm not like most girls."

"No, you are not."

Adrian swallowed hard in the ensuing silence.

"That's why," Laura said as she reached across the table for Adrian's hand, "I think you're good for Jake, and if you ever doubt that or his Riley stance gets to be too much for you, don't ever be afraid to come talk it out with me okay."

"Okay." The confidence in her voice surprised Adrian.

She felt like she had just received a blessing from the pope, and she did take Laura up on her offer several times and, Adrian did have to admit, it was nice to talk to someone who knew exactly what she was going through.

A horn blared somewhere on the street below, disrupting Adrian's thoughts. She looked at her camera. Photographic evidence of her husband with his guard down could be locked inside there. Adrian shoved the newspaper out of her way; she couldn't wait to get started.

Adrian was just about to pull the memory card from her camera when the telephone rang. She tilted her head backward and sighed. She really didn't want to go back inside, but she also knew it might be something important.

"Hey, Adrian; it's Laura. I'm sorry for calling you so early, but I wanted to catch the two of you before you left for work."

"Well, you caught me, but you just missed your son by about ten minutes," Adrian replied.

"That's all right. I'll just pass the info on to you, and you can relay it to Jake for me."

"Sure. What info is that?"

"The info about dinner tonight for the four of us at Valentino's. I made the reservation for seven. I hope that's not too late for you guys."

Adrian nearly dropped the phone onto the kitchen counter. She raised the palm of her hand to her forehead and let it slide slowly down to her cheek.

Oh, shit! Dinner tonight! The four of them! How could I have forgotten about that?

"Oh...no," Adrian winced. "Seven should be fine."

"We are still on for tonight, right?" Laura asked anxiously.

"Oh, yeah. Sure."

"Good. You had me worried there for a minute. I thought maybe you were going to cancel on us."

"Oh, no, no. We'll be there." Adrian made a face.

I would've cancelled if I had remembered agreeing to it in the first place.

"Okay," Laura responded happily. "We'll see you tonight."

"Okay, see you tonight." Adrian tried to imitate her mother-in-law's cheerfulness, but fell short.

Adrian shut off the cordless phone before she took the receiver and repeatedly hit her forehead with it.

Oh, shit! Jake was going to kill her.

It wasn't that he didn't like going out to dinner with his mom. He did. The problem was going out to dinner with his mom and her boyfriend, Clint.

Chapter Two

Laura shook her head in disappointment after she hung up the phone. Adrian was lying to her, again. Laura should've known better than to expect anything else. There was no way in the world Jake would accept a dinner invitation from them, much less be looking forward to it. It hadn't happened in seven years, but that didn't stop Laura from believing it couldn't happen someday.

Laura's eyes drifted over to the collage of framed photographs that hung on the wall beside the staircase. Each spot held a small school picture of her son from first through eleventh grade, with his senior picture placed prominently in the center. She smiled wistfully up at it.

Jake, in the earlier pictures, smiled broadly as if he were the happiest kid in the world. That smile diminished slightly from year to year and had been replaced by a scowl tainted with attitude in his graduation photo.

Laura sighed heavily. She wondered whether her son's transformation would've been nearly as drastic if his father hadn't died during his freshman year of high school.

Her hand instinctively went to her wedding ring that she wore as a necklace. She fondled it while she shut her eyes and remembered that day. It was as clear to her as if it had just happened yesterday instead of eleven years ago.

It had been a weekday: Monday, April 22 to be exact. Laura woke up early and was already busy multitasking. She emptied and reloaded the dishwasher, checked her e-mails, then shouted up to Jake every five minutes or so to get out of bed so he wouldn't be late for school. Laura needed to watch the time too. She had to be at the pizzeria to meet the delivery truck that was supposed to arrive there first thing that morning.

She checked her watch before she added another chore to her to-do list for the day, just as a commercial came on the small flat screen TV. A frazzled mom complained about how her family never had time to eat together anymore. That is, until she found these fabulous quick-and-easy homemade meals in some magazine she claimed every mother should subscribe to.

Laura's head popped up. She didn't care about the meals or the stupid magazine. What got her attention was when she heard the mom say she was tired of her family eating all of their meals inside their minivan.

Laura stared shamefully at the Pop-Tart in her hand. Their typical morning meal. Jake ran so late most days that he'd just snatch the Pop-Tart from her before they both rushed out to the car.

Sure enough, Jake flew down the stairs moments later as if he were trying to outrun a fire. He reached for his Pop-Tart, only to have his mom pull it away from him.

"Hey," Jake exclaimed, "what did you do that for?"

"Change of plans," Laura answered while she dialed the phone. "We're going to eat breakfast together this morning."

Jake looked at her as if she were crazy.

"What," she asked after she saw the look her son was giving her, "you don't want me to call school and give you the morning off?"

"Whatever."

Jake's backpack dropped like dead weight from his hand as he flopped down onto the nearest chair. Once Laura finished talking to the school secretary, she called every one of her brothers until she got one of them to go meet the delivery truck for her.

"There, our schedules are cleared. So now, what would you like? I'll make you whatever you want."

"I don't care," he responded before he grabbed the remote and started channel surfing.

"Oh...okay."

Laura's voice fell like a deflated balloon. Jake must've picked up on it.

"Waffles," he suddenly muttered.

"What?" she asked as she poked her head out of the refrigerator.

"You said I could have whatever I want," Jake shrugged. "I want waffles. Unless it'll take too long."

Laura tried to contain her excitement. "No, no. We've got plenty of time."

He finally settled on a station to watch. She kept one ear tuned in to the hot topics that came up on SportsCenter while she mixed the batter just in case she heard a conversation starter she could use on him.

If there was one subject Laura was well versed in, it was sports. She had to be, growing up in a family with five brothers. So Laura had no trouble talking to her son about whom the Packers should choose as their first-round draft pick, then switch seamlessly over to which team had a real shot at bringing home the Stanley Cup if the situation ever called for it.

This morning was no exception. ESPN did not disappoint; the co-anchors were in a heated discussion about who should be the MVP of the NBA, which led to a light-hearted argument between mother and son.

This was nice, Laura thought even though nothing she said could change Jake's mind about how great Shaquille O'Neil was. *We'll have to do it again soon, like the next time Kevin's home.*

Jake changed the channel as soon as a commercial came on while Laura poured some of the batter into the waffle iron.

She hadn't paid any attention to what Jake turned on, until he suddenly asked her where exactly in Texas his dad was driving through.

Laura glanced at the corkboard map of the United States that hung on the wall across from her. They had been using it to keep track of Kevin's routes ever since Jake was a little boy. It was filled with different colored pins that stretched from one coast to the other. The code was fairly simple: red pins indicated where Kevin had already been; green the route he was currently on.

Laura stepped up to the map and squinted at the state of Texas until she found the right pin.

"Houston," she said casually.

There was a long pause before Jake said anything.

"Are you sure?"

The tone of his voice made Laura nervous, but she wasn't about to let Jake know that. It was probably nothing. She double-checked the map. Yep, Kevin was in Houston.

Jake didn't say a word.

"What?" Laura asked as she rushed to his side. "What happened?"

Still, Jake said nothing.

Laura put her arm around her son while she stared wide-eyed at the television screen.

A breaking news story had interrupted the regular morning newscast. Fog was the cause of a horrific pile up that had happened earlier that morning on I-10 in Houston, Texas. The young female reporter on the scene declared it the worst traffic accident that had happened in the state in nearly a decade.

Laura felt her entire body go numb. All she saw on the screen were miles and miles of charred, twisted metal that no longer resembled vehicles of any kind. Smoke and flames overtook the darkened sky. There was no way for Laura to know whether her husband was even involved in the accident, but she didn't need proof. She felt it. Kevin was gone and, from that moment on, her life changed forever.

Chapter Three

Laura devoted most of her time and attention to Jake after Kevin's death. Too much if you asked her family and friends. The longer that devotion went on, the more concerned they became about her. So they did the only thing they could think of to help her: They pushed her back into the dating pool.

Laura knew they all meant well. She even humored her brothers by going out on a couple of blind dates they set her up on. All it ever did was confirm the obvious, at least to her anyway. She wasn't ready and, truth be told, she didn't know whether she ever would be. Laura tried to explain this to everyone but they just didn't get it. Kevin had been the love of her life. She had never wanted to be with anyone else, especially after he died, and the thought of starting all over again just sounded too damn exhausting to her. And then there was Jake.

He hated the idea of his mother dating anyone. He never said so, but he didn't have to. Laura saw it in his eyes on those rare occasions she did go out. Jake always looked at her with such contempt. Her son made her feel as if she were doing something wrong, like she was cheating on her husband somehow. The guilt from that alone was enough to keep her permanently single.

So love was the furthest thing from Laura's mind on the day she met Clint Walker.

She had been up to her elbows in pizza dough when Jake's school called. Her older brother Vinnie held the cordless phone up to her ear so she could listen to the principal's secretary tell her the bad news.

Jake was a good boy, but he'd been attracted to trouble from the moment he learned how to walk. That wasn't so much of a problem back when his father was still alive. All Laura had to do was threaten to call him and Jake's attitude instantly adjusted.

But she couldn't do that anymore. She was on her own now, and she had absolutely no idea how to rein her son in.

Laura tried to talk to him, but all of their conversations ended in fights. There was even a dent in the living room wall from where his fist had landed.

Jake had stormed out of the house after that particular battle royal. Laura spent half the night driving all over town looking for him. She spent the other half reciting the rosary at the kitchen table until her son finally came home around the crack of dawn.

Jake stood at the front door without the slightest trace of remorse, reeking of alcohol with a police officer by his side.

The cop let Jake off easy, but he warned him that he might not be so lucky next time. This did more to scare Laura than it did Jake. She prayed to God every day after that to give her the strength she needed just to get her son through high school.

Jake was only a couple of weeks into his senior year when the call came from the principal's office.

"Jesus, Jake!" Laura fumed after she got off the phone.

"What did he do now?" Vinnie asked.

"Well," Laura sighed, "this time your nephew supposedly told his English teacher to go fuck herself."

"Nice," Vinnie replied sarcastically.

"Do you mind taking over for me here?"

"Don't worry about it. Just go, and try not to kill anyone, especially old lady Horowitz."

"I can't promise anything," Laura responded with a grin as she dried off her hands and raced out the back door.

Principal Horowitz—or old lady Horowitz as she was better known by the students—had been at East Side High School forever. Laura and all of her brothers had had her for a principal; she was horrible back then, and aging only seemed to have made her worse. Laura dreaded going in to see her even now. She still felt like a kid herself every time she went in to discuss Jake, and she always left feeling like the world's worst parent.

When Laura trudged through the door of the principal's office, however, she was startled to find a younger, attractive man sitting behind old lady Horowitz's desk.

Laura did a double take. She thought maybe she was in the wrong room for a moment until she saw Jake slouched back in a chair in front of her. The man stood up as soon as he saw her.

He was in his early forties and tall—about 6'5"—with light brown hair shaved close to his head. He wore a pair of dark blue jeans, and the sleeves of the light blue pin-striped dress shirt he wore were rolled up to his elbows. He extended his hand to her in introduction, and much to Laura's surprise, she caught herself checking out his ring finger, which she was thrilled to find bare.

"Mrs. Riley," he said cordially, "I'm Clint Walker; the new interim principal."

"Please," she responded with nervous laughter, "call me Laura."

Oh, my God, Laura thought, *did I really just do that?*

She must've because Jake glared at her in disbelief. The funny thing was this time she really didn't care what her son thought.

What is wrong with me?

Mr. Walker was explaining to Laura why Principal Horowitz had to resign so suddenly, but all Laura could concentrate on were his emerald green eyes.

She barely heard a word he said. Laura grinned from ear to ear when they left the principal's office, as if she had just been told her son was selected as valedictorian instead of being suspended for a week.

They ran into each other again when she brought Jake back to school. Mr. Walker told her if she ever needed any help with Jake or just wanted someone to talk to, to give him a call.

Laura eventually took him up on his offer. She tried to convince herself it was nothing more than a concerned parent speaking to her son's principal, even though a small part of her hoped for more.

Their school meetings turned into coffee; coffee turned into a bite to eat, and the next thing Laura knew, Clint was asking her out on a real date.

The chemistry between the two of them was undeniable. Laura had to admit she loved spending time with him. He made her feel so at ease, like they had known each other forever. Clint also genuinely cared about Jake. That's why they both agreed nothing more could happen between them as long as Clint was the principal of Jake's high school.

Everything came to a head the summer Jake graduated. Laura and Clint officially started dating, which didn't sit well with Jake at all. This led to one of the worst fights she and Jake had ever had.

Laura fell asleep at Clint's house and stayed the night. She snuck in the next morning with her high heels in hand. Her plan was to get to her room before Jake woke up, but it failed. He reached the foot of the stairs at the same time she crossed the threshold of the front door. Laura stood frozen in place and waited for the inevitable fallout.

Her son looked her over—from her tousled hair down to the same dress she'd had on when she left the night before—with an accusing eye. He scoffed.

"Jake," Laura said remorsefully.

"Save it," he replied.

"Jake, please."

"I bet you just couldn't wait, could you?"

"Watch it, Jacob," she warned him. "You may be eighteen now, but I am still your mother."

Her words fell on deaf ears.

"You were probably just counting down the days weren't you, until you could finally fuck the principal!"

Laura couldn't believe what happened next. It all happened so fast that later she thought maybe she had imagined it, but she felt the sting in her palm and saw her fingers trembling afterward.

Laura's lips quivered while she reached out to touch Jake's reddened cheek. He pulled away and tore upstairs.

Jake moved in with one of his uncles for the rest of that summer. Laura feared she had lost him forever, but they eventually worked things out. Jake was civil to Clint whenever he had to see him after that, but Laura knew deep down her son would always resent him.

Laura stared nervously down at the diamond ring she wore on her left hand.

"Please God," she prayed out loud, "help Jake find a way to accept this."

*

Adrian breathed a sigh of relief when they pulled up to the restaurant. It had been one of the longest trips to the east side of town she had ever taken.

She caught a glimpse of her husband out of the corner of her eye. Jake sat in the passenger seat of the Saturn with his arms folded over his chest. He hadn't changed position or spoken a single word the entire way there. He reminded her of a child forced into taking a time-out.

Adrian shook her head as she shifted the car into park. She could normally tolerate her husband's bad behavior, but for some reason, he was working on her last nerve tonight.

She would never understand why Jake still held such a grudge against Clint. Clint was a good guy. He and Jake's mom had been together for a long time now, and they both seemed very happy, but none of that mattered to Jake. Adrian usually never got into it with him about this, but she was pretty damn close now.

She handed the keys to their car to the valet and glanced over her shoulder at her husband who still hadn't moved.

"You coming?" she asked him.

"I hate this," Jake grumbled as he stared straight ahead of him.

Adrian wanted to take him and shake him; scream at him to get over it. To tell him just to suck it up and be a man like he usually did, but she bit her tongue.

Why makes things worse?

"I know," she said with as much sympathy as she could possibly muster. "But it's just dinner. How bad could it be?"

*

Valentino's Italian Bistro was an upscale restaurant about fifteen minutes outside of town and secluded deep within the northwoods. As Jake and Adrian walked through the brick oval entranceway, their eyes were immediately drawn to the mural of the canals of Venice that dominated one wall. Dean Martin crooned "That's Amore" through the sound system. Jake shut his eyes while he breathed in the enticing aroma of freshly baked garlic bread. All seemed to be right with the world until he saw them.

His mother and Clint sat at the far end of the polished oak bar, waiting for them. Jake's demeanor instantly changed. He clenched his fists; his jaw set. He looked like he was ready to do battle.

Adrian gave Jake's hand a supportive squeeze, but his body language remained the same.

The only time Jake seemed to relax at all was when he greeted his mom. He embraced her warmly, and then he exchanged an awkward handshake with Clint.

"Our table's not ready yet," Laura informed them. "Do you guys want something to drink while we wait?"

"Absolutely," Jake answered a little too eagerly.

Adrian tugged lightly on his arm.

"Just a Sprite for me, please," Adrian told the bartender. Laura stared curiously at her daughter-in-law. "I'm driving," Adrian explained.

"Oh…okay," Laura replied skeptically. "Jake, what are you having?"

"A Bud Lite, and keep 'em coming." Jake muttered this last part to himself as he turned his attention to the TV above the bar. Adrian heard him and yanked his arm so hard she nearly knocked him over.

Jake bit down hard on his lip and attempted to remain calm.

Jake's mom reached for her drink; Adrian gasped when she saw it.

"What? What's wrong?" Jake asked.

Adrian glanced nervously at Laura. Laura pleaded with her eyes not to say anything just yet.

"Nothing," Adrian stammered. "I...uh...just thought I saw this gigantic spider on the bar, that's all."

"Uh-huh, sure," Jake responded doubtfully. "Now you want to tell me what's really going on?"

"Did you guys hear that?" Laura interjected. "I think they just called our name. Our table must be ready."

"I didn't hear anything," Jake said.

He searched up and down the bar until his eyes zeroed in on his mother's left hand. Laura tried to hide it, but she wasn't fast enough.

"What the hell is that?" Jake asked her.

"What?" Laura asked.

"On your finger. Is that what I think it is?"

Laura looked anxiously back at Clint.

"Go on," he told her with a supportive nod. "Looks like the cat's already out of the bag anyway."

"Oh, Jake," Laura began as she placed her hand back up onto the bar, "this is so not how we wanted to tell you this."

Jake didn't say a word. He just stared grimly at the ring on his mother's left hand.

"Jake," Clint began, "your mom wanted you to be the first to know about this. That's why we asked you and Adrian to come here with us tonight—so we could all celebrate together."

"Celebrate?" Jake asked as his eyes locked onto Clint's. "Really?"

"Jake," Adrian begged.

Jake shook his head incredulously at them before he set his beer down and marched toward the door.

"Where are you going?" Adrian asked him.

"Home," Jake answered flatly without looking back.

Adrian threw her head back in defeat. Her first instinct was to chase after her husband, but she reconsidered when she saw the look on Laura's face.

Laura stared dumbfounded at the door that her only child had just exited through. Clint wrapped his arms around her and kissed her gently on her forehead. Adrian reached for her mother-in-law's hand.

"Don't worry about me," Laura told her. "You just go take care of him."

Adrian ran outside, fueled by anger, to find Jake pacing back and forth along the sidewalk. He hooked his index finger into the collar of his dress shirt and ripped it open just as the valet pulled up with their car.

The young man was about to hand Jake the keys when Adrian snatched them away from him.

"Oh, hell no!" she said.

"What?" Jake replied.

"You are not driving anywhere!"

Jake rolled his eyes. "Adrian, please." His words came out slow and deliberate. "Not now. I have to get out of here."

"Fine, but I'm driving."

They stared each other down for what felt like an eternity.

"Just drive fast," he eventually conceded.

*

Jesse Higgins stood in the center of the basketball court in his gray tank top and baggy blue shorts. His hands rested on his knees while the sweat poured off his long brown hair. He was playing one-on-one against his best friend, Matt Cline, and losing badly.

"All right," Jesse panted, "I give up. You win."

Matt stood underneath the net, shirtless, with the ball tucked into the crook of his arm as if he were posing for the cover of *Sports Illustrated*.

"My mad skills were just too much for you today, hey?" Matt asked with a victorious grin.

"Mad skills?" Jesse mocked his friend while he straightened up. "Nah, that was just me giving in and letting you win."

"Yeah, right," Matt laughed. "That's why you look like you need to be carted off in an ambulance from exhaustion."

Jesse flung his moist towel at his friend on their way to the bench. Matt ducked, even though the towel was nowhere near his head. Jesse drained his bottle of Gatorade before they grabbed their duffel bags and headed out to the parking lot.

"Well," Jesse said, "at least I have a better ride than you do today."

Matt stopped cold.

"You're kidding, right?" he asked as his eyes darted from his 1979 Trans Am to the shiny brand new Ford Mustang parked beside it. "You really think your dad's mid-life crisis mobile is better than my vintage car?"

"Your car's not vintage," Jesse snickered. "It's old. I could blow the rust off it right now if I wanted to."

"Oh, you think so?"

"I know so."

"Enough to put your money where your mouth is?"

"What did you have in mind?"

"I'll bet you double or nothing my old Trans Am can take your daddy's Mustang out on the freeway. What do you say?"

Double or nothing did sound pretty good to Jesse. He could save face from his disastrous showing on the basketball court, plus hold bragging rights over Matt forever if the Mustang could really pull it off.

"You're on."

*

Tension filled the inside of the Saturn. The only sound came from the engine humming. Adrian drove down Bay Settlement Road, her eyes focused on the traffic in front of her. She was so pissed off at Jake right now that she couldn't even speak to him. Not that he would have heard a word she said anyway.

Jake sat in the passenger seat and refused to look at his wife. He gripped the arm of the door so tightly that the veins in his arm started to protrude. The only thing that caught his attention was when she missed their turn onto Church Road.

Neither one of them said a word. Adrian felt Jake's eyes pierce through her, and it only made her angrier. Now they were going to have to drive all the way around town.

Great. Just great.

*

They were fast approaching the on ramp to I-43. Jesse had all the windows rolled up and the air conditioning on full blast. The adrenaline pumped through his veins well before he slid his Queen CD in.

Jesse adjusted the Bluetooth in his ear before he called Matt.

"You still back there somewhere?" he teased him.

"I'm right on your ass, man," Matt instantly shot back.

"Not for long."

Jesse pressed down on the accelerator and merged effortlessly onto the freeway. He moved one lane over so that he and Matt could be right alongside each other.

"So, when do we start?" Matt asked him.

Jesse smiled wide. His lane was clear while Matt had a few vehicles in front of him to contend with. The timing couldn't have been more perfect.

"Now!" Jesse answered.

He blew past Matt doing at least eighty miles per hour. Jesse pictured Matt's mouth dropping wide open at that very moment.

"You son-of-a-bitch!" Matt said to him, semi-impressed. "I never knew you had it in you!"

Jesse just laughed to himself as he cranked up the volume on his stereo so loud that the drum section of "We Will Rock You" practically blew the glass out of all the windows.

*

Jake still had his eyes trained on Adrian. She couldn't hold it in any longer.

"What?" she blurted out.

"Nothing," Jake mumbled.

Adrian saw him shake his head from side to side.

"If you have something to say to me, just say it already," she told him.

Jake let out what Adrian thought to be an over-exaggerated sigh. "You don't understand."

And that's when she lost it.

"You're right," she said. "I don't."

She turned to him. The last time he ever remembered seeing her eyes this wild was on the day he had first met her.

"I don't understand," she continued, "how a grown man can continue to act like such a spoiled, selfish little brat!

"You're not a kid anymore, Jake. Yes, your dad died and it was a horrible thing, but that was seven years ago! Get over it already! I am so sick and tired of walking on eggshells around you whenever the subject of your mom and Clint comes up.

"Tonight was supposed to be a celebration, but you managed to turn it into yet another train wreck. How much longer are you going to keep this up? Until your mom's dead and gone too? When are you finally going to let her be happy? She deserves that, don't you think?"

Adrian's body shook uncontrollably. Jake tried to put a comforting hand on her shoulder, but she brushed him off. His arm fell back into his lap like dead weight.

"We need to get off here," he told her coolly.

*

The race was a close one. Matt eventually caught up to Jesse, and then the two of them traded the lead several times as they weaved through the traffic.

"You ready to give up yet, man?" Matt asked him.

"We'll go to the next mile marker. Whoever is in the lead then is the winner," Jesse replied.

"Sounds good to me."

Jesse begged the Mustang to give him everything it had, and it responded. He and Matt were neck and neck on the freeway when, just inches away from the mile marker, Jesse found a last blast of life that sent the Mustang out in front of the Trans Am.

"Yes!" Jesse exclaimed as if he had just won the Daytona 500.

"Good job, man," Matt told him. "I am impressed."

"Must be my lucky day."

"Got to be. No other way to explain it."

*

Adrian caught Jake rolling his shoulders back and sitting up straight as an arrow. Now it was her turn to shake her head.

"Of course," she spat out in disgust. "The God-damn, frigging Riley response again! Can't you ever do anything else?"

Adrian struck a nerve. Jake slammed his fist down so hard on the dashboard that she nearly jumped out of her seat.

"There!" he shouted. "Would you rather see more of that instead?"

Adrian felt hot tears brimming in her eyes, but she willed them not to come out.

"No," she muttered. "I'd rather just get home."

His anger instantly subsided, replaced now with heartfelt guilt.

"Adrian," Jake beseeched her, but he got nothing in response. "Sweet thing," he tried again. He reached out to stroke her cheek, but she turned sharply away from him before his fingers could even brush her skin.

Jake sighed in frustration, and resigned himself to focusing on the highway in front of them.

Adrian!" he screamed, realizing the lane they were in was rapidly coming to an end.

"Jesus Christ!" she replied.

Adrian cranked the wheel hard to the left to get onto I-43 in time. She didn't check behind her for traffic—never saw the black Mustang that barreled down upon them. It was too late for Jesse to do anything except brace himself for the worst.

Matt watched in horror from the far left lane as the Mustang plowed into the Saturn and rammed the car into the concrete guard railing.

The collision was gut-wrenching to anyone who heard it, but the worst sound came from the deafening silence that followed.

Chapter Four

Cassie had just left the hospital cafeteria with her bottled water when her cell phone buzzed. She pulled it out of her jacket pocket to see who it was. Then she stopped dead in her tracks in the corridor, unsure whether she should ignore the call or answer it. She chose to ignore.

Her relationship with her parents had become strained, to say the least, ever since she had chosen EMT training over law school.

Cassie had always dreamt of becoming a lawyer. She was well on her way to turning that dream into reality too, until the summer she and Adrian worked as lifeguards.

There had been a frightening moment. A young boy had jumped off the high-dive board and not come back up out of the water. Cassie had dived in after him while Adrian frantically dialed 911. They had performed CPR on him until the EMTs arrived.

Cassie had then sat back on the wet concrete astounded. She watched the paramedics swoop in all cool and confident while they helped save that child's life as if it were just another day at the office. That piqued her curiosity. She needed to learn more about this profession.

Cassie did her homework. She spent most of her days off at Mercy Hospital. She researched the position and spoke to as many EMTs and their trainers as she could. Her mind was made up by the end of the summer.

Her decision didn't go over well with her parents. They thought she was being rash—that it was a phase, like gymnastics and horseback riding lessons, that she'd grow out of as soon as she entered law school. Cassie insisted they were wrong. Her parents told her she was throwing her life away. They even threatened to cut her off financially. Cassie said that was fine; she was perfectly capable of taking care of herself.

Their conversations became few and far between after that, which made this call all the more baffling.

Cassie fidgeted with her cell phone.

What if something's wrong, or maybe—just maybe—they've finally come around?

Yeah, right.

That's when Cassie's pager went off. She needed to get back to the ambulance. They were being called to a Code Blue.

Her feet couldn't move fast enough. Her partner, Max—a veteran EMT—was ready and waiting for her behind the steering wheel when she reached the ambulance.

"You ready to roll?" he asked her.

"Let's do it," she answered with a confident nod.

Cassie strapped herself into the passenger seat. She put her earphones in, shut her eyes, and zoned out to Miranda Lambert while Max weaved through the heavy traffic. This wasn't the first Code Blue Cassie had been called to, but she still reacted the same way every time.

In the beginning, her mind had gotten caught up in a whirlwind of rational and irrational thoughts. Max had taught Cassie early on to find something that calmed her down. Music was the only thing that quieted the chaos inside her head.

But today was different.

She pulled her earphones out as soon as they arrived at the scene.

"Holy shit." She sounded like she was talking in slow motion.

"C'mon, Cass," Max said. "Clock's ticking. We need to move."

"Right. Sorry."

Rule #1, Cassie reminded herself, *Focus on your job. No matter what.*

Cassie jumped from the ambulance. Her jaw dropped while she tried to process the wreckage that surrounded her.

The freeway's on ramp and the majority of the right lane were closed down. The left lane was jammed with vehicles. The majority of their occupants nearly broke their necks trying to get a better view of what happened.

How ironic, Cassie thought. *Here I am with the best seat in the house for a show I really don't care to see.*

She looked up to watch the sun fade into the horizon. Its golden rays spread wide across the sky like a warm, comfortable blanket while black smoke rose up to meet it from the remains of the intertwined vehicles.

"Oh, what a wonderful world," she mumbled sarcastically to herself.

"Cass, move your ass! Now!" Max said.

Focus, damn it. Focus!

She raced over to Max.

"What do you need me to do?"

"I need you to help me get this kid out of this car as quickly and carefully as possible. It looks like the air bag deployed, but we won't know how serious his injuries are until after we get him out of there."

*

Cassie heard a young male voice in the background while they worked.

"That car! It just came out of fricking nowhere! It all happened so fast. There was nothing he could do! It wasn't his fault! It wasn't his fault!"

Stay focused. Keep your mind on your work.

"The race was over," he continued remorsefully. "He beat me. He won. He fucking won."

Tune him out. Just tune him out.

They cut the driver free from his seat belt and placed him gently onto a stretcher. He was conscious. He knew his name and where he was, and he asked a million questions.

Cassie tried to calm him down. "It's okay; everything's all right. Just relax."

"What about the people in the other car? Are they okay?"

Cassie didn't miss a beat. "Everyone is fine," she told him, even though she couldn't say for sure whether that was true. "Let's just concentrate on getting you better, okay."

She and Max were wheeling him over to their ambulance when she heard someone cry out. The voice sounded so familiar to her that she couldn't ignore it.

Cassie let go of the rail on the stretcher. She moved toward the other victim as if someone had poured concrete around her feet. Her ears were deaf to the sound of her partner screaming his lungs out at her.

The victim held tight to her wrist as soon as she reached him.

"Cass," he gasped, "is she okay? Please, tell me she's okay."

Cassie felt like she had just gotten the wind knocked out of her as she stared down into Jake's bruised and bloodied face. Everything around her suddenly zoomed into sharper focus. Her eyes darted from Jake, to the remains of the silver Saturn, to the nearest paramedic who gave her an ominous shake of his head. The color drained from her face when she saw the coroner zip up a long, black body bag.

She looked like a lost soul standing there. All of her training, everything she had learned, went right out the window. No words could bring her back into the game now.

"What the hell are you doing, Adler?" Max snapped at her.

Cassie opened her mouth to speak, and that's when the floodgates opened.

"I know them," she sobbed. "They're my friends."

"Oh, Jesus," Max replied as he draped a comforting arm around her. "C'mon; let's get you back to the hospital."

Cassie nodded while Max led her back to the ambulance. All she could think about was that her best friend was gone.

*

Cassie sat in one of the hard plastic chairs in the emergency waiting room. She wrapped her arms tightly around her as if she were freezing. Her right leg jittered uncontrollably; her eyes locked onto the sliding door of the main entrance. There was still no sign of them. She leaned her head back and stared up at the ceiling.

It still wasn't registering. Part of Cassie hoped this was all just some horrible nightmare or a terrible mistake. Maybe she had heard the name wrong, jumped to the wrong conclusion, and the woman who died really wasn't Adrian at all. Cassie's optimism faded fast when she saw Laura.

Laura charged into the room like a bull attacking a matador. Clint was just a step behind her.

"Where's my son?" Laura demanded from the poor unsuspecting admitting nurse.

"Laura," Clint told her gently, "calm down."

"Oh, God," Cassie mumbled to herself while she crouched down in her chair. *It wasn't a mistake or a nightmare; this is really happening.*

Cassie overheard the nurse tell them that Jake was in surgery right now and that he was in stable condition. Laura let out a sigh of relief before she asked her next question.

"And Adrian, his wife. How's she doing?"

Cassie cringed and wished she could've been anywhere else but there at that moment. Luckily, her cell phone distracted her.

She fished it out of her pocket and realized her parents had been trying to get a hold of her for a while now.

They must've heard about the accident.

Normally, Cassie would've just sent them a quick text to let them know she was okay. When she looked at Laura, who had fallen into Clint's arms, she realized she couldn't do that this time. Her fingers shook as she dialed the number.

"Mom? Hey, it's Cassie." She paused while her mother spoke on the other end. "Yeah," Cassie agreed. "I'm glad to hear your voice too...."

Chapter Five

A drian felt dazed and confused, as if she were stumbling around in a fog.

Where the hell am I?

She shut her eyes to avoid the blinding white light and was terrified to open them again, but once she did, she was treated to the most amazing sight.

An awe-inspiring array of colors splashed across the vast horizon in front of her.

I have to photograph this!

She felt frantically around for her camera, but it was nowhere to be found.

Where is it? Where's my camera? I need to find my camera!

Panic rose to its highest level inside of her as she sped toward the horizon, but the closer she got to it, the calmer she became. Adrian tipped her head back in relief and was prepared to be embraced by it when a collision of voices suddenly erupted behind her.

Adrian whipped her head around.

Something's wrong, very, very wrong. I need to find out what's going on!

She was drawn to the voices, each one more intense and urgent than the next. The horizon and all of its enticing colors were a distant memory. All Adrian could concentrate on now was one very familiar voice that silenced all the rest.

"My wife. How is she?"

"I'm all right," Adrian answered.

She was by her husband's side before she could even finish her sentence. Adrian had no idea how she got there so quickly and, to be honest, it really didn't matter. The only thing she cared about right now was Jake.

He looked awful lying in that hospital bed. He seemed so vulnerable and weak.

"Oh, my God," Adrian exclaimed as she cupped her hands around her mouth.

Jake's eyes narrowed while he gingerly pushed himself up on the bed. "What's wrong?" he asked. "Why won't anyone answer me?"

A look of confusion spread across Adrian's face as she slowly lowered her hands. "I just did, Babe."

Jake didn't respond to her. He looked past her to the doctor who stood alongside his mother and Clint. All three seemed very uncomfortable, and none of them could look Jake in the eye.

"Jake," the doctor began, "you really do need your rest."

"I'm not tired," Jake replied adamantly. "I just want to know how my wife is!"

"I just told you," Adrian said a little louder this time as she reached over to pat his arm. "I'm fine."

The palm of her hand went right through her husband's arm, and all Adrian felt was air. She jumped back in shock, but no one else in the room reacted to it.

"What the...? She gasped before she turned toward the other people in the room. "What the hell just happened?"

No one answered her because none of them even seemed to notice she was there. Adrian waved her hand in front of the doctor, but he didn't even flinch.

"What's the matter with all of you?" Adrian shouted. "Why is everyone ignoring me?"

"They're not," someone else answered her. "They just can't see you anymore."

She looked to the back of the room where a man leaned against the wall with his arms folded across his chest.

He looked good for a man his age—late forties, early fifties, Adrian guessed. He stood at least six feet tall, with thick, wavy blonde hair that curled around the nape of his neck. He had a smooth, clean-shaven face. And the man was built. His arms in particular seemed to be pure muscle.

There was something else about this guy too. Adrian couldn't place him, but she swore she had seen him somewhere before.

He wore a gray T-shirt, a pair of well-worn blue jeans, and brown work boots. He gave her a sympathetic smile as he took a step toward her.

"Who are you?" she asked.

He chose his words carefully as he approached her. "I was sent here to help you with your transition."

"Transition?" she repeated. "To what? I don't understand. None of this is making any sense."

"It will," he replied, "soon enough."

Adrian tried to fire more questions at him, but he silenced her by raising his index finger to his lips so they could watch the rest of the scene unfold in the hospital room.

Laura turned away from her son. She didn't want him to see the tears that welled up in her eyes, but he still heard her stifled sobs.

"Mom," Jake said, his voice filled with irritation, "what's the matter?" Laura couldn't speak. "Would someone please just tell me what the hell is going on?"

The doctor sighed. This was the absolutely worst part of his job. There was no easy way to say it, but it had to be said.

"Jake," he began, "your wife—"

"Adrian," Jake interrupted him.

"Adrian," the doctor repeated. "She sustained a very serious head injury from the accident. It sounds like her side of the vehicle received the most damage, and even with the airbag and her seat belt…well, it was still very touch and go."

"But she's all right, right?" Jake asked.

The doctor stared somberly down at his chart. "We rushed her into emergency surgery and did absolutely everything we could, but there was still a lot of internal bleeding that we just couldn't control."

Adrian saw her husband's jaw clench and his face harden. "No," he said angrily. "No!"

"I'm sorry, Jake," the doctor said sincerely, "but your wife is gone."

Chapter Six

Adrian turned back to the man who stood beside her. "If this is a joke," she told him, "it's not very funny."

"It's no joke," he answered.

"All right." Her voice betrayed her nerves. "This has got to be a dream. Some really horrible nightmare I'm about to wake up from at any second."

"I'm afraid not."

"So what's going on?"

He looked compassionately at her. This was the absolutely worst part of his job, but it had to be done. There was no easy way; he just had to come out and say it. "You died, Adrian."

She scoffed. "No, I didn't."

"Yes, you did." He paused while he tried to think of the best way to explain it to her. "Remember when you tried to touch Jake's arm and your hand went right through him? You're no longer flesh and blood. You're a spirit now."

Adrian stood dumbfounded while his words sunk in. She stared wistfully at her husband, wanting nothing more than to be wrapped inside his arms, but she didn't know whether that was even possible anymore.

Adrian needed to know for sure, so she inched toward the bed.

"Adrian, are you all right?" the man asked as he followed her.

She exhaled slowly before she laid her head on her husband's chest.

Tears trickled down her cheeks while she eagerly anticipated Jake's hand on the back of her head. Adrian hoped upon hope that his fingers would gently stroke her hair the way they always did whenever she had a bad day. She held onto him so tightly that she was afraid she might be hurting him more. Adrian wept once she realized her husband's arms were still lying motionless at his sides.

The man called out Adrian's name just as Laura said her son's.

"Just leave me alone!" Jake and Adrian both replied.

Laura, Clint, and the doctor all obeyed Jake's request, but the man ignored Adrian and remained standing alongside Jake's bed.

"What?" Adrian asked, her voice filled with frustration. "Now you can't hear me anymore either?"

"I can still hear you," he answered. "I just can't leave you."

"Yes, you can!" Adrian shouted as she sat up to face him. "There's the door," she pointed furiously. "All you have to do is walk to it and get the fuck out!"

"I'm sorry." He folded his hands in front of him, his eyes cast downward onto the floor. "But I can't."

"Why not?" Adrian shoved him harder than a defensive lineman trying to sack a quarterback. "Just get the hell out and leave me alone!"

She wanted to knock him on his ass, but she went right through him as if he weren't even there. Adrian lay on the cold tile floor and stared up at the man in shock.

"How did you do that?" she stammered. "Who are you? What are you?"

"It's okay," he responded as he leaned down to help her back up.

"No! Don't touch me!" Adrian protested while she crawled backwards to the door.

It's okay," he said again. "I'm here to help you."

"I don't need your help."

"Yes, you do. And so does Jake."

Adrian looked over at her husband. The light of the moon shone through the window and onto his grave face, which revealed a darkness within him that terrified her.

"He's hurting," the man told her. "He needs to grieve."

"He won't," she replied with bitter sarcasm, "because real men don't grieve."

Adrian stared curiously at the man while he cleared his throat.

"You know," she said, "you still haven't told me who you are."

"C'mon, Adrian. Isn't it obvious?"

She followed his gaze onto Jake. Her eyes darted back and forth between the two men until she finally saw it. The same unique shade of blue colored both men's eyes. How could she not have seen it before?

"Oh, my God." She spoke each word with shocked slowness. "You're Jake's father!"

Chapter Seven

Jake wasn't a picture person. That had always been Adrian's department. He never felt the need to display personal photographs, but he did have a few that he kept to himself.

Adrian discovered them one night back when she and Jake were still dating. They were horsing around in his apartment. She wanted to see what was in his wallet, and he kept playing keep away from her by holding it high over his head. Jake had a good five inches over Adrian, but that still didn't stop her from snatching the wallet out of his hand.

"Ah ha!" she exclaimed triumphantly. "Now, let's see what you've got in here, young man."

"C'mon, Adrian; just give it back to me."

"No way, not until I see what's inside."

They continued to wrestle with each other until she got the wallet open with a flick of her wrist.

"Ah, what's this?" she teased him. "Pictures."

Only two photographs were tucked behind his driver's license. The first was of him and her. It was a little blurry, but Adrian recognized it right away. Mardi Gras at The Borderline.

They sat at the bar wearing party hats and layers of beads around their necks. Jake had his arm draped over Adrian. They were cheek to cheek. Their faces lit up from more than just the alcohol.

"Awwhhh," Adrian cooed. "That was our six-month anniversary."

"Okay, that's enough pictures for tonight."

"Ah, c'mon, Jake. You've got to let me see the other one now. Please."

"Fine." He took a step back. "Go for it."

This photograph was older and faded. A man held a little boy in front of him on a motorcycle. The boy was small. His legs just barely hung over the seat as he lunged forward to grab hold of the gigantic handlebars. Their smiles were the same but different. The boy's was one of pure joy, while the man's came from sheer pride.

"Who's this?" Adrian asked.

"That's me and my dad," Jake answered quietly. "My mom took that picture of us on the day my dad bought that motorcycle. It's a chopper with a 110cc engine and a wide 280 back wheel." Adrian stared blankly at him as if he had just spoken to her in Russian. "The motorcycle of his dreams," he translated.

"Oh, gotcha. So what happened to it?"

"She's mine now." Jake paused for what seemed like an eternity to Adrian. "I keep her tucked away in storage for safe keeping until I get the itch to go out for a nice long ride."

This time, Adrian didn't put up a fight when Jake reached for his wallet. She let him take it out of her hand and put it inside the back pocket of his jeans. That was the one and only time she had ever seen either one of those pictures, but they still stuck with her.

That's where Adrian had seen this man before, in the picture. He was the one holding Jake.

He was Jake's father.

"You can call me Kevin," he told Adrian.

"There are a lot of things I'd like to call you," Adrian said while she stared daggers into his extended hand, "but Kevin isn't one of them."

"Oh, I can just about imagine," he said as he withdrew his hand. "Can't say that I blame you either. I deserve to be called every foul-mouthed, four-letter word you can think of."

Adrian stared skeptically at him. "So what? Is this the part where you tell me you've seen the error of your ways or something?"

"Let's just say I've learned a lot about myself since I died."

"Oh, really," Adrian said with a roll of her eyes, "like what?"

"Like," Kevin began reluctantly, "maybe my way wasn't the best way to raise my son."

"Gee, you think?"

He raised an eyebrow at her. "I've seen what it's done to Jake, and I tried to get through to him before you got here, but I couldn't. And now I'm afraid it might be too late."

"What are you talking about?"

"What I mean is, my death hit Jake really hard, but that was nothing compared to what losing you will do to him if we can't help him through it."

Adrian's jaw dropped; her face lost all of its color. Kevin spun around to see what she was looking at.

Her husband was shrouded in darkness. But that wasn't the only thing that scared Adrian.

"I can hear him," she told Kevin.

But Jake hadn't said a word.

Chapter Eight

"It's all right," Kevin told her.

"What's happening to me?" Adrian asked.

"You're hearing his thoughts," Kevin explained. "It's perfectly normal."

"Yeah, maybe for you it is."

"Just listen to him."

"Listen to him," Adrian repeated incredulously. "Okay."

Adrian's gone? No. No way she's gone. She can't be. She was just sitting right beside me in the car.

Wait. She was driving the car. Shit! She drove because she didn't want me to. She thought I was too angry to drive, and I was, so I gave her the keys. No, she made me give her the keys. That was the only way she'd let me leave, and I had to get the hell out of there, so I just gave them to her, but she got pissed off at me anyway. Really pissed off. I've never seen her so angry before.

"It's true," Adrian said, more to herself than to Kevin. "I don't know what came over me. Normally, I can keep my opinions to myself about him and his mom, but not this time. I just lost it on him."

She was yelling at me instead of paying attention to the road. I tried to warn her but it was too late....

"Oh, no," Adrian said. "He's blaming himself. Now what do I do?"

"Convince him otherwise," Kevin answered.

"And just how do you suggest I do that?"

"By talking to him."

"He barely listened to me when I was alive; what makes you think anything's going to change now?"

"Your belief in him."

Adrian swallowed her attitude like a bitter pill.

"What do I do?"

"You do whatever feels right."

"Okay."

Her voice caught in her throat while she moved, without thinking, onto the bed and into her husband's arms.

Listen to me, Adrian began as she looked up into his eyes and caressed his cheek. *This is not your fault. I don't blame you, so please, babe, don't be putting all the blame on yourself. It's not going to do you any good, and it's certainly not going to bring me back. If you're going to do anything for me, focus all of that energy on getting yourself better instead. Please.*

Adrian's eyes fell hopelessly away from Jake's, but she kept talking to him until she heard her own words inside his mind.

"Holy...!"

Adrian would've crashed onto the floor if Kevin hadn't been there to catch her.

"I knew you could do it," he told her.

Their victory was short-lived; the negative thoughts returned with a vengeance.

It is my fault. None of this would've happened if I would've just kept it together. I'm the one who blew up. I'm the one who had to leave. Why didn't she just let me go? Why did she have to chase after me? Why did she insist on driving? You know why.

I never should've let her drive. Not that I would've done much better. Hell, neither one of us should've been behind the wheel. We weren't even supposed to be anywhere near that damn, fucking freeway! We were supposed to be having dinner, but I just couldn't keep my big mouth shut.

She died because of me. I killed her.

Adrian's eyes widened as those thoughts overtook her own inside Jake's head and the darkness intensified around him.

"What's happening?" Adrian asked fearfully.

"There's a war going on inside of him right now—a battle between good and evil, and it's up to you to make sure that the right side wins."

"Me? How?"

"Just keep doing what you're doing."

"But it's not working!"

"It will; it has to, for him."

Adrian turned helplessly back to her husband. She was supposed to have all the answers, but she had nothing. The darkness seemed to snuff out what little light remained.

Adrian heard Jake's heart pounding. She glanced at the monitor beside him. His blood pressure was off the charts.

I don't know what I'm supposed to do! She put her hands to her temples and rubbed them furiously. *Oh, God, what am I going to do?*

Meanwhile, images of Adrian filled Jake's mind. He shut his eyes, but she was still there, larger than life, and there was no escaping what he imagined her saying to him:

You killed me!

Jake couldn't take any more. The darkness consumed him. He sat up and ripped the IV out of his arm. Alarms sounded and machines went crazy.

"No," Adrian roared. "I'll be damned if I'm going to let you die because of me!"

She poured her heart and soul into the kiss she gave Jake, in the hopes it would be enough to keep him fighting.

Adrian sat back, breathless and exhausted, while a team of doctors swarmed around him.

"Come on," she urged Jake, her eyes fixated on the monitors until his heart rate returned to normal.

"Hard work saving a life, isn't it?" Kevin asked her.

"Mm-hmm," was all Adrian could manage to say.

*

Adrian heard something that jolted her awake. She looked around but saw no one, not even Kevin.

Oh shit! The darkness is coming back again!

"No," Adrian said as she thrust her arms out to the sides like a barrier to protect her husband. "I won't let you take him!"

The door creaked open. Panic filled Adrian's lungs and constricted her voice.

"You're still here."

Adrian doubled over in relief when she realized it was Clint.

"I can't leave; I just can't; not yet."

The light from the hallway revealed Laura's silhouette. She sat in a deep chair and focused solely on her son.

"He's going to be fine," Clint reassured her.

"You don't know that. You don't know how he's going to feel when he wakes up and remembers Adrian's gone. He can't be alone when that happens. I won't leave him alone..."

"Honey, please, calm down."

"What if he feels like I did after Kevin died...?"

"Don't."

Kevin's voice startled Adrian.

"Kevin? Where are you?"

"Please, Laura," Kevin continued, "do not go there."

Adrian squinted into the darkness and followed the sound of his voice. She found him on his knees before Laura, his hand over hers.

"Don't go where, Kevin?" Adrian asked. "What happened after you died?"

Her words fell on deaf ears. Kevin was in another world, lost in the moment with his wife. Adrian suddenly felt as if she were intruding on a very private moment.

Chapter Nine

Laura's Vibe crept up to the front of the house. She put the car in park and killed the engine, but neither one of them got out. Laura watched her son stare warily out the passenger side window at his upstairs apartment.

"You know you don't have to stay here if you're not ready."

Jake didn't respond; he didn't even turn away from the window.

Laura swallowed hard before she continued. "You could always come stay with us."

The stone cold stare Jake gave his mother was harsher than any four-letter-word he could've used in front of her.

"Or not," Laura mumbled.

An awkward silence fell over them while Jake's eyes drifted back to the house.

Adrian and Kevin sat right behind Jake in the backseat. Adrian flung her arms around her husband's shoulders and tightly shut her eyes. Kevin looked at her as if she were crazy.

"What are you doing?" he asked.

"This is it," Adrian answered. "He's going to let go right now. I can feel it!"

Laura put her hand on Jake's shoulder. He shrugged it off and immediately yanked on the door handle. Laura sighed heavily before she got out of the car.

Adrian slumped back in her seat.

"I know you were hoping for a miracle," Kevin tried to console her, "but look at him."

Adrian leaned forward. Jake's left arm was in a sling, and he winced every time he moved, but he still fended off his mother's attempts to help him to the front door.

"His bullheadedness is stronger than ever," Kevin said. "That's going to take a lot more than a bear hug to fix."

"But how?" Adrian asked.

"That, my dear, is the million-dollar question you and I need to come up with the correct answer to."

"Great. No pressure at all," Adrian replied while she watched her husband struggle up the stairs.

Jake's momentum stalled once he reached the front door. He put the key in the lock and wouldn't let go. His eyes were so intent upon it that they could've burned a hole through the metal.

"What do you think?" Kevin asked her. "You ready to give it another shot?"

Adrian hung back, her arms crossed. She shook her head.

"No? Okay, suit yourself."

Kevin put his hand on Laura's elbow. She instinctively reached out to cover Jake's hand with hers, and together they opened the door.

Adrian's mouth fell open.

"How did you do that?" Adrian asked him.

"Well, first off, you don't need to be so overdramatic," he teased her. "And secondly, it had way more to do with their free will than anything I could've done."

They fell silent when Jake took a step backward. Laura placed her hand on his back and gently nudged him forward.

Jake couldn't get over it. Adrian was everywhere; in the pictures that hung in the hallway, the old wooden rocking chair she just had to have in their living room, and in the photography magazines that lay scattered across the coffee table. There wasn't anything in this apartment his wife hadn't left her mark on.

Jake lowered his head and closed his eyes.

Stop, he thought to himself. *Please, just stop.*

But they wouldn't. The memories kept coming like raging flood waters through a broken dam.

He remembered carrying her over the threshold of this apartment for the very first time as husband and wife only a year ago. He had pretended to lose his grip on her and said he might not be able to make it all the way down the hall to their bedroom. Adrian had played along with him.

"Well, what do you suggest we do?" she asked.

Jake wiggled his eyebrows and smiled mischievously before he lay Adrian down on the floor beneath him.

"Stay here until I can work up the energy to bring you to bed," he answered.

"Sounds good to me," she said as she wrapped her arms around his neck and brought his lips down closer to hers. "Honestly," she added right before they kissed, "I wouldn't mind if we never made it to bed tonight."

Bed. Jake stared dreadfully down the long hallway toward their bedroom. He wasn't sure whether he could ever go back inside that room again.

"This is too much for him," Adrian objected.

"No, it's not," Kevin argued.

"All right, that's it," Laura said suddenly. "You are not staying here alone tonight, and that's final."

Jake's body instinctively snapped into the Riley stance while his father's voice echoed in his ears:

Real men don't need anyone to take care of them. A real man can take care of himself.

"Mom, I'll be fine," Jake replied.

"No, you won't be." Laura reached up to cup her son's chin in her hand and force him to look her in the eye. "This is a hard thing for anyone to go through, and no one, not even your father, would expect you to handle it alone."

"Did it ever occur to you that maybe I don't want anyone around me right now?" Jake asked as he broke free from his mother's grasp.

"Jake."

"Mom, please, don't."

"Fine," Laura huffed, "but I'll be here first thing in the morning to help you get ready for the funeral."

"Fine," Jake responded coldly.

She was about to leave. Her hand was on the doorknob when she stopped. "I love you, Jake."

This had become a habit of hers ever since his father had died. She couldn't leave without saying "I love you" to him. It also made it extremely difficult for him to stay angry at her.

"I love you too, Mom," he responded sincerely.

"I'll see you tomorrow," she said as she shut the door behind her.

*

Jake stood there with the palm of his hand pressed up against the doorframe and peered into the darkness.

It's just a room, he tried to convince himself. *Four walls. Nothing more.*

But there was more. This was their room—his and Adrian's—and he couldn't go any farther than the doorway. It was crazy, but Jake swore her scent wafted through the air as if she were standing right next to him.

"It's all right," Adrian said while she took her husband's hand and tried to lead him inside.

Jake felt his chest tighten. He inhaled sharply before he turned on his heel and headed back down the hallway.

Adrian's hand fell listlessly to her side.

"C'mon; shake it off," Kevin told her.

She nodded somberly before they went into the living room.

*

Jake slept on the hide-a-bed that night, if he could even call what he did sleep. He lay on his back, his eyes wide open.

Adrian curled up in her favorite antique rocking chair and frowned at her husband. Kevin glared at her.

"Go to him," he told her.

"Why? I'm useless to him," Adrian moped.

"Oh, please. That's enough of this self-pity crap. Get up and go to your husband. Now!"

"And do what?"

"What you normally did when the two of you went to sleep. C'mon; he needs you."

"Yeah, right."

"Just do it. Please."

"Fine."

She flopped down beside Jake.

"Really? You look like you're lying on a bed of nails."

Adrian scowled at Kevin, but she didn't change her position. Jake suddenly rolled onto his side, his arm draped over her.

Adrian stared anxiously down at it until Jake pulled her close. She couldn't resist curling into him; it felt so good.

Hmmm...maybe this isn't such a bad idea after all.

Jake's dreams were wonderful to begin with. His wife was alive and lying right next to him, talking his ear off because she wasn't tired. He rolled over and pulled his pillow over his head. She giggled and only spoke louder.

Then Adrian heard the rain falling outside. She sprang from the bed, ran to the window, and flung the drapes wide open.

"There's a storm coming!" she shouted gleefully. "C'mon; we need to be out in it!"

"It's the middle of the night," Jake groaned.

"Please, for me," she begged.

"Oh, all right, but you're driving."

The next thing he knew, they were on the freeway in the middle of downtown Chicago. There were no other cars on the road, and the rain beat down upon the ground. Thunder roared and the lightning briefly lit up the skyscrapers that surrounded them. Jake was nervous, but the worse the storm got, the more excited Adrian became.

"Where's my camera?" she asked him.

"Are you sure you should be doing this while you're driving?" he asked as he handed it to her.

"Don't worry; we'll be fine."

Just then, a bolt of lightning zigzagged across the sky directly above them. Adrian stopped the truck right in the middle of the intersection.

"Wow, these pictures are going to be so awesome!" Adrian exclaimed.

Her eyes were to the sky, oblivious to the black Mustang that came out of nowhere and hit them head-on. Jake's screaming shattered the silence in the apartment.

"What the hell was that?" Adrian asked Kevin while she comforted Jake. "That's not the dream I wanted him to have!"

"You have to remember," Kevin explained to her, "that there are two sides to his conscience. We're not the only ones working here."

"The darkness."

"Mm-hmm."

Adrian stared gravely at her husband. He couldn't seem to catch his breath, and his entire body was drenched in sweat. She couldn't allow the darkness to do this to him.

"C'mon, babe," Adrian said while she stroked his back. "Remember the good rain.

"Remember when we drove down to Chicago for my cousin's wedding? I was one of the bridesmaids, and I warned you that if I had to dress up, then so did you. You hated it—I know you did—especially when I dragged you to that Men's Warehouse in the mall on playoff Saturday, but you never made a big deal out of it, at least not in front of me anyway. I got to admit, though, you looked damn fine in that gray suit and lilac-colored tie that matched my dress."

Adrian giggled. "I'm surprised we even made it to the reception."

She paused. Jake lay back down and fell asleep; his mind drifted back to the same moment in time that Adrian was in.

They drove to the reception in Jake's truck; they were halfway to the banquet hall when the sky suddenly changed from a bright summer afternoon to as black as the ace of spades. The wind blew and thunder rumbled off in the distance. Jake quickly rolled up his window.

"What are you doing?" Adrian asked, disappointed.

"There's a storm coming," Jake replied.

"Yeah."

The giddiness in her voice amused Jake.

"What?" Adrian asked embarrassed. "I can't help it. It's all my dad's fault. I used to be terrified of thunderstorms when I was a kid until he convinced me they were rock concerts from heaven." She grinned. "And I've been chasing the music ever since."

"Well," Jake replied good-naturedly, "I hope you'll forgive me if I listen to this performance with my window up."

"Your loss," she shrugged.

He laughed as Adrian hung her head out the window and drew in the hot, humid air as if it were the most enticing scent in the world.

"What?" she asked after she caught him looking at her.

Jake smiled fondly at her. "You're crazy. You know that, right?"

Adrian smiled back at him as the rain began to fall. "And you love me for it, don't you?"

"Absolutely."

"So you won't mind pulling over by Buckingham Fountain for me?"

Jake cocked his head to one side and stared incredulously at her. They were downtown, the traffic was horrible, and they were already late for the reception. He was just about to argue those exact points to her when he saw the look in her eyes. Then all logic went right out the window.

"No, I guess not," he conceded.

"Thank you," she exclaimed while she wrapped her arms around his neck.

It took some doing, but Jake finally managed to work his way through the congested traffic to the fountain. He parked the truck alongside it and waited. He figured Adrian would just take some pictures and they'd be on their way again, but she had other ideas.

"C'mon," she told him as she reached for her door.

"Are you serious?" Jake exclaimed. "It's pouring out there."

"Aw, c'mon," Adrian teased him. "You're not scared of a little rain, are you?"

"No," he replied defensively.

"Then come on," Adrian insisted while she kicked off her black stiletto heels. The thunder roared louder and longer like an ominous drum roll. "Did you hear that?" she asked excitedly.

"Yeah, the storm's getting worse."

"No, they're playing our song!"

Jake rolled his eyes at her. "I am not dancing with you; not now, not in this weather."

Adrian ignored him. She ran around the front of the truck to the driver's side door and stood there with an exaggerated frown on her face, her hands folded in prayer.

"Please," she begged him.

"This is nuts," he said as he opened his door. "We could get struck by lightning."

"Not a chance."

Adrian led Jake up the steps to the fountain. The rain chilled him to the bone. All he wanted to do was get back into the truck and crank up the heat until Adrian placed his right hand on her hip, looped her arm around his waist, and pulled him to her. He watched their fingers intertwine in fascination while they swayed slowly back and forth to whatever made-up tune Adrian hummed along to.

Jake barely noticed the multicolored lights of the fountain or heard the people yelling and honking their horns at them from the cars that raced by. He was too caught up in the moment to care about anything else.

Jake pushed Adrian away from him and twirled her around before bringing her right back into his arms. Adrian stared at him, wide-eyed.

"I love you," he told her.

Adrian beamed. "I love you too."

Jake brushed the wet strands of hair away from her face with his fingertips. Their mouths met in a passionate kiss just as a bolt of lightning illuminated the sky above them.

"I think that's our cue to leave," Jake said.

"Yeah," Adrian agreed, "I think you're right."

"That's what I wanted you to remember," Adrian told her husband now, "instead of that nightmare you had to endure."

Jake woke up just as she rose from the couch.

Damn stupid dreams, he thought. *First that nightmare and now this one about Buckingham Fountain. How the hell am I supposed to get any sleep?*

"What do I do?" Adrian asked while she watched Jake stumble into the kitchen.

"Follow him," Kevin told her.

Jake headed straight for the fridge for a cold beer; the first thing he saw when he peered inside was Adrian's gallon of chocolate milk. His mouth went dry; he wasn't thirsty anymore. When he shut the door, he immediately caught sight of her mug.

Adrian couldn't take her eyes off it either. She sat behind him on the edge of the counter, oblivious to the fact that Kevin had disappeared.

"It's still right where I left it," Adrian said, her voice bittersweet.

"It was the night we met your mom and Clint for dinner," she continued. "We were running late. I gulped that chocolate milk down as fast as I could. Set that mug right there on the counter instead of in the dishwasher, even though I knew how much you hated that."

Adrian and Jake both remembered what Adrian had promised him: *I'll take care of it later, when we come back home.*

She watched her husband place the massive mug in the palm of his hand. He ran his thumb slowly over it as if he were rubbing a magic lamp.

But she never came back home, Jake thought.

Jake felt a huge lump rise up from the pit of his stomach and lodge in his throat. He tried to suppress it, but it proved to be too difficult for him to swallow.

Adrian eagerly awaited his reaction. It wasn't what she expected.

A primal, agonizing scream erupted from deep within Jake's soul as he wound up his arm and threw the mug as hard as he could. Adrian curled up into a ball as it smashed against the kitchen wall.

Just then, Jake heard someone pounding wildly on his door.

Chapter Ten

"Jake!" Laura shouted frantically as soon as she heard the crash. "Jake, open this door right now!"

He glanced up at the clock on the wall and groaned.

What the hell is she doing here at this time of night?

"Jake!"

"All right, Mom; calm down," Jake finally responded. "I'm coming."

Thank God the downstairs neighbors are out of town, he thought, *or the cops would be here next.*

"What the hell is going on in here?" Laura interrogated him as soon as he opened the door.

"A glass broke," he mumbled while he rubbed the back of his neck. His eyes never once met hers.

"A glass broke," she repeated, unconvinced. "C'mon, Jacob. Really? This is me you're talking to here."

Jake sighed in frustration. "Yes, Mom. Really."

"Don't lie to me."

"All right, I won't. It's the middle of the night, and I'm too damn tired to fight with you right now."

"So why weren't you sound asleep in your own bed?"

Jake didn't have an answer for that one.

Laura regretted the words as soon as she said them. "I'm sorry. I'm just worried about you; that's all. Something told me to come over here tonight and check on you, and I'm glad I did."

Adrian glanced suspiciously at Kevin.

"What?" he asked innocently.

"You were the something, weren't you?" Adrian asked him.

"I plead the Fifth on that one," Kevin answered, raising his hand up in the air as if he were about to swear on the Bible.

"Well, you've checked on me, so now you can go right back home," Jake told his mother.

"Oh, no," Laura protested. "I'm not going anywhere."

"I really don't need you to sleep over, Mom."

"It's not up for discussion, Jacob."

Jake's eyes widened in disbelief while he watched his mom set off to find a broom and dustpan.

"Don't worry about me," she said later as she swept the floor. "You just go lie down and get some rest."

"Mom," he objected.

"Jake," Laura immediately cut him off, "you just said you were tired; now go back to bed and lie down."

He didn't move. Laura glanced at him. She saw a flicker of apprehension in his eyes even though he was trying his damnedest to hide it.

"Although I suppose you're probably wide awake now that I barged in on you, huh?" she asked him.

"Huh?" Jake answered in confusion.

"But I bet if you stretched out on the hide-a-bed and turned on the

TV, you'd be able to find something to put you to sleep, like a Bears documentary on ESPN or something."

Jake gave his mom a knowing smile. She pretended not to see the tension ease from his face.

"Thanks, Mom."

"Anytime, hon," she replied nonchalantly while she continued to clean up the kitchen.

Laura waited until Jake was out before she went into the living room to sit by him. It reminded her of when he was little and he'd have nightmares. Kevin had never allowed Jake to sleep between them at night, so Laura would have to sneak into her son's room after they tucked him back in. She would snuggle up beside Jake in his cramped little twin bed, her arm half numb from him lying on it, until all the monsters had disappeared and he slept peacefully once again.

"Did you know that?" Adrian asked Kevin after hearing Laura's thoughts.

"I had my suspicions," Kevin answered, "but I never knew for sure until now."

Laura collapsed into the old rocking chair. She pulled the multicolored afghan off the back of it to wrap up in and, for the first time in a long time, sat in the darkness and watched her son sleep.

Her eyes had begun to droop when she heard Jake say something.

"I love you, sweet thing," he mumbled while he rolled over and let his arm fall onto the empty pillow beside him.

Oh, sweetie, his mother thought, *I wish I could slay this monster for you. But it's all up to you this time.*

*

It was still dark when Laura stretched her tired, aching muscles. She placed her hand on the back of her neck and tried to rub the kinks out, but it was a lost cause. Well, what did she expect after spending an entire night sleeping in a rocking chair? She got halfway up, then stopped to watch her son for just a moment longer.

Laura saw that blissful look on Jake's face and knew right away he was dreaming about Adrian. The same thing had happened to her for months after Kevin died.

They were the sweetest dreams Laura had ever had. They were so vivid and real she'd wake up believing he was still alive. Then reality would seep in like lead being poured into her heart. She couldn't wait for the night to come just so she could be with her husband again. It even got to the point where all Laura wanted to do was sleep.

"Jake, I hate to do this to you," she said as she stood up, "but you've got to wake up."

Laura went over to the window and thrust the curtains open. Jake groaned and turned away from the light, but she wasn't finished yet.

"C'mon; rise and shine, sleepyhead!" Laura shouted as she yanked the blankets off him.

"Knock it off, sweet thing," Jake mumbled, still half asleep. "My, God," he continued while he clawed at the blankets that weren't there, "the birds aren't even up yet!"

Laura stood speechless for a moment.

Sweet thing? Oh, my God. He thinks I'm Adrian.

"C'mon, Jake," Laura said, gentler this time, while she rubbed his shoulder. "It really is time to get up."

"Since when did my sweet thing become such an early bird?"

He reached for Adrian's hand, and was startled to find his mother standing over him instead.

"Mom! What are you doing here so early?"

Laura cleared her throat. "I...uh...stayed here last night, remember?"

"What? Why?" he asked as he sat up and rubbed the sleep from his eyes.

Words failed Laura, but fortunately, she didn't need any. She watched while her son slowly took in his surroundings.

Jake scanned the living room. He ran his hands along the thin lumpy mattress just as his eyes locked onto the lone pillow beside him. He inhaled sharply.

"Jake, you okay?" his mom asked.

Laura caught a glimpse of the sorrow in her son's eyes, but it vanished as quickly as it had appeared.

"Yeah," Jake replied as he got up from the hide-a-bed, "Yeah, I'm fine."

"Are you hungry? I can make you something to eat. Anything you want."

"No thanks, Mom," he muttered while he trudged toward the hallway.

"Where are you going?"

"I need to get ready," he answered flatly. "Take a shower."

Laura sat back down in the rocking chair. She shut her eyes and mumbled something to herself over and over again that Adrian couldn't understand.

"What is she saying?" she eventually asked Kevin.

"The Lord's Prayer," Kevin answered.

Laura didn't stop until she heard the sound of bare feet padding against the hardwood floor. She opened her eyes and saw her son standing humbly before her dripping wet with a towel wrapped around his waist.

"C'mon," she said. "I'll help you find something to wear."

Chapter Eleven

A drian couldn't believe what a gorgeous day it was outside. The air smelled sweet, the sky was a startling blue, and the possibilities seemed endless. Unfortunately, the only thing she had to look forward to on this perfect summer day was her own funeral.

She and Kevin walked down the sidewalk toward St. Gregory's Catholic Church. The traditional white clapboard church stood on a spacious corner lot surrounded by nearly identical suburban homes. Everything about the church was beautiful, but what attracted Adrian the most was the pristine white steeple that rose up from the front of it. She tipped her head back and shielded her eyes with her hand as she looked up to the very top where the huge iron bell hung. A smile crept across her face as the memories came rushing back.

Adrian had grown up in this church. She went to parochial school here from the time she was six years old until she started high school. She saw herself racing up those steep stone steps in her black patent leather shoes and red plaid school uniform in a desperate attempt to make it to morning Mass before that bell chimed throughout the entire city.

There was something else about that bell tower too, something Adrian hadn't thought about in a long time. It had happened on the night of her eighth grade graduation. She and Tommy Shaw had snuck up there to carve their initials into the bell with the Swiss army knife Tommy's dad gave him as a graduation present. That was also the night Tommy asked Adrian to go steady with him. She said yes without hesitation, and seconds later, received her very first kiss. It didn't last long, though. Sister Helen caught them and dragged them downstairs for face-to-face confession with Father Martin.

Adrian's face instantly reddened, which didn't go unnoticed by Kevin.

"So, you and Tommy Shaw, huh?" he teased her.

She turned to him with a look of disbelief on her face.

"Sorry," Kevin shrugged, "but your thoughts are not your own anymore."

Just then the bell rang, and that's when Adrian finally took notice of it all. Cars filled the parking lot while a black sea of mourners flooded the entrance to the church. Adrian gasped as she covered her wide-open mouth. She had expected a lot of people, but nothing had prepared her for this.

"C'mon," Kevin said while he put his arm gently around Adrian's shoulders. "Let's go inside."

All Adrian could do was nod as Kevin led her through the front door.

The church seemed darker than the last time Adrian had been inside it, despite the light that illuminated the stained glass windows. She accompanied her casket down the aisle along with the pallbearers. Adrian ran her hand over the brown, polished, mahogany surface, mystified by the fact that she was standing there while her body lay trapped inside that box.

She came to an abrupt halt once she reached the pew her parents were in.

Adrian had always known Abbey and Craig Cattrel to be so...alive. To see this version of them—two prematurely aged, depleted souls comforting each other as best they could—nearly destroyed her.

Don't cry! Do not shed one single, fucking tear!

Adrian whipped around the second she heard her husband's voice.

Adrian had seen Jake in his Riley stance a million times before, but this was the first time he had ever struggled to sustain it.

She wanted desperately to hold him, but she was afraid her touch might break him.

C'mon, man; you've got to keep it together for just a little while longer, Jake kept telling himself.

That's when Adrian noticed how badly her husband's hands were shaking.

"It's all right," she told him.

No, I need to be strong for everyone else.

"But what about you?"

Jake closed his eyes and tried to block everything out. Adrian took a chance; his hands stilled as soon as she put hers around them.

Thank God, Jake thought. *My Riley strength came through for me again.*

Adrian felt like she had just gotten the wind knocked out of her. She let go of Jake and ran out of the church so fast that she almost plowed right into her best friend.

Adrian had to do a double-take. She stared incredulously at the frail young woman who hovered anxiously in the vestibule—her fair complexion now a ghostly pale.

"Cass?" Adrian asked.

Cassie peeked inside and inched forward, but faltered.

I can't. I just can't do this.

She snuck out of the church with Adrian hot on her heels.

"Cassie, wait! Come back!" Adrian shouted.

But it was too late. Cassie had already disappeared inside the back of a waiting taxi cab.

Adrian sat on the steps of the church with her head in her hands. She heard the front door ease open and knew, without even looking back, that it was Kevin.

"Don't even," she warned him. "I'm in no mood to hear any inspirational words of wisdom from you right now."

"I wasn't going to say any," Kevin replied as he sat down beside her.

"Good, because I'm…."

Adrian lost her train of thought after she raised her tear-streaked face up to meet Kevin's.

"Whoa," she said. "What happened to you? You look worse than I do."

"Yeah…well…" he stammered.

"Laura?" she asked hesitantly.

"Yeah," he admitted, "Laura."

"Damn." Adrian winced. "Sorry. I was kind of hoping you'd tell me there was some kind of supernatural cure for that."

"I wish I could," Kevin chuckled, "but there's no cure for that kind of pain."

"Great," Adrian groaned.

"It sucks, I know, but it's good that we feel that." Adrian raised a skeptical eyebrow at him. "Because it reminds us how much we love them and would still do anything for them, no matter how much it hurts."

Adrian arched an eyebrow at him.

"What?" he asked.

"Dying really changed you, didn't it?"

Kevin shrugged.

"C'mon; suck it up now," he said as he tapped her leg with the back of his hand. "We've got a party to get to."

"Or not."

*

Adrian leaned back against one of her living room walls to watch the endless procession of people who had come to pay their respects to Jake. It broke her heart to see them all look at him as if he were some kind of wounded animal lying helplessly on the side of the road, but it didn't seem to affect Jake at all.

His Riley stance served him well. He even hugged and consoled some of those who were there to comfort him, but Adrian knew better.

She saw the dullness in his eyes, felt the void in his heart, and heard how everyone sounded to him like adults in a Charlie Brown cartoon.

Well, almost everyone.

A woman's voice got through to him—someone he didn't recognize, but Adrian did.

"My Auntie Valerie."

"It doesn't make any sense to me at all," Valerie said to Jake. "We were just at your wedding reception, and now this. It's not right. It's just not right. You two deserved to have a long, happy life together."

Those words were just enough to topple the wall of grief that built up inside of Jake. He managed to numb himself to the pain, but now it had awakened like a sleeping bear, its grip on him so strong that he felt like he couldn't breathe.

"We've got to get him out of here," Adrian told Kevin.

"Do not make a big deal out of this," Kevin instructed his son. "Just get to the door, any door, as quickly and calmly as possible."

"I agree," Jake responded to Valerie. "I'm sorry, but I need to step out for a minute and get some air."

Jake made it out to the balcony without incident.

She's right, he thought. *None of this makes any sense. Why,* he asked, his eyes raised up to the sky, *did you fucking have to take her from me now? Why couldn't you have waited? Let us have just a little more time together. Just give me one good fucking reason why you had to have her now?*

"I'd love to hear the answer to that one myself," Adrian said.

She felt her husband's eyes on her before she saw them.

Adrian leaned forward in her white wicker chair in anticipation.

And then, just like that, with a shake of his head, whatever Jake thought he had seen or heard was gone.

Adrian fell listlessly back into her seat while Jake stormed over to the railing.

"Goddammit!" he yelled as he tried to beat the hell out of it.

"Hey, I know you're going through a lot today man, but don't take it out on the railing; it's just trying to support you."

Jake looked behind him, his eyes narrowed at his best friend. Charlie stood by the door and shrugged.

"I couldn't help it," Charlie explained. "I had to lighten the mood somehow."

Jake still didn't look amused.

"Hey, it could've been worse. You could be dealing with your mom right now if I hadn't convinced her to let me come out here instead."

"I guess it can't hurt to let him think he convinced her, huh?" Adrian asked Kevin.

"Not at all," Kevin agreed.

Jake peered over the railing. There was no way out. His truck was blocked in by all the well-wishing mourners.

Great. Just fucking lovely.

"You know," Charlie said with a hint of nervousness in his voice, "I can still go get her if I need to."

"Relax," Jake replied as he ran his hands through his hair. "I just have to get out of here; I need to ride, but there's no way I can get my truck out to get there."

"Oh," Charlie's voice flooded with relief. "Now that I can help you with, so long as you don't mind walking a little way to my truck."

"Lead the way, man."

Jake and Charlie strolled back inside a few minutes later, oblivious to the frantic whispers and prying eyes that followed them along with Jake's anxious mother.

"Jake," Laura stopped her son as discreetly as possible in the hallway, "is everything okay?"

"Yeah, I'm leaving," he responded calmly.

"Leaving?" Laura lowered her voice. "Why?"

"I need to ride."

Laura saw the look in her son's eyes and pushed him no further.

"All right. You go do what you need to do."

"Thank you."

"Just be safe. Please."

"I will."

Chapter Twelve

Adrian sat in somber silence in the back of Charlie's truck. She knew all about Jake's riding. It had been something he had done ever since his dad had passed away. It was his release; one of the few things that calmed him down. She wondered why she had never thought of it before.

"You okay?" Kevin asked. "You're awfully quiet over there."

"I'm fine," she replied softly.

Kevin studied Adrian warily. He knew what "fine" meant in a woman's vocabulary.

"It's not your fault, you know," he told her.

"What?" Adrian asked dazed.

"It wouldn't have changed anything if he came here instead. It was just your time, Adrian."

"I know," she mumbled, still lost in her own world.

Adrian stared out the window and watched Charlie turn into the storage facility. They drove all the way to the back, hung a left, and rolled slowly down the aisle until Jake told Charlie to cut the engine in front of one of the units.

"Thanks man," Jake told him as he jumped out of the truck. "You're a life-saver."

"Anytime," Charlie replied.

Jake stood outside in his dark suit and waited for his friend to drive away. Then he dug into his pants pocket and pulled out his wallet as he made his way to the door. Jake produced a small silver key that fit perfectly into the lock. He grabbed the handle and hoisted the garage door.

Jake paused, his arms still raised above his head, before he stepped purposefully inside and removed the tarp.

Jake had seen it a million times before, but it always left him in awe. Adrian turned to Kevin, who seemed to have fallen under the same spell as his son. All she saw was an old motorcycle, but she knew it meant much more to them.

Memories of him and his father and this motorcycle hit Jake hard. He saw his dad balancing him on the seat of this bike while he pretended to drive it when he was just a toddler; their first real ride together. All the weekends they practically lived in the garage working on it whenever Kevin made it home from the road.

"There's a lot of history in this bike, huh?" Adrian said to Kevin.

Kevin pried his eyes away from his motorcycle to stare curiously at Adrian.

"What?" she asked self-consciously.

"He never took you out on this bike, did he?"

"Nope, but I never wanted him to."

"Why not?"

"I don't know," she shrugged. "It just never felt right to me. That time on the bike was his, you know, sort of like whenever I locked myself in the bathroom to take a nice, long, hot bath. I didn't want to intrude."

"What about now?"

"Huh?"

"Why don't you go for a ride with him now?"

"What? No!"

"Trust me; you won't regret it. And I think it'll do you some good too."

"I'm not so sure about that," Adrian replied while the bike roared to life.

"I am. Now go."

"All right, all right. I'm going."

Kevin chuckled as he watched Adrian hang onto Jake for dear life.

"You know you have nothing to worry about, right?" he reminded her.

"I know," she answered semi-confidently.

"Just have fun."

"What about you? Wouldn't you rather go?"

"Nah," Kevin replied while he stared wistfully at his bike. "This is your ride."

Adrian buried her head in Jake's back as they took off out of the storage facility.

"Relax," she heard Kevin's voice in her ear. "Open your eyes; look around you; take it all in."

Adrian pried one eye open, then the other as they sped down the highway. She sat up straighter and loosened her grip as she channeled into Jake's passion for that bike.

The cool wind whipped Adrian's hair around and stung her face, but it felt amazing to her. The sweet summer air filled Jake's lungs and freed his cluttered mind. That's when Adrian finally understood.

This is Jake's thunderstorm.

"I got it, babe."

Adrian rested her chin on Jake's shoulder. Jake smiled broadly as he remembered his wife with her head out his truck window during that storm in Chicago.

Adrian shrieked with delight when Jake stepped on the gas pedal. They raced forward with no particular destination in mind.

Time seemed irrelevant while they were riding. Before Adrian knew it, they were crossing the Sturgeon Bay Bridge and heading into Door County. The only reason they stopped was for gas and food.

Jake parked alongside a beach. Adrian sat side-saddle on the bike while he leaned against it and scarfed down a chili dog he ordered from a nearby food truck. Tons of sunbathers trouped past them in their flip-flops and designer swimsuits, but the one thing they both became well aware of was all the families. Everywhere they looked, there seemed to be mothers and fathers chasing their children through the sand or splashing around with them in the water.

Jake tipped his head back and shut his eyes as a memory hit him like a migraine.

Adrian had come out of the bathroom holding a pregnancy test in her hand; her disappointment was written all over her face. It had been maybe two months after they got married.

He took her in a warm embrace as she shook her head from side-to-side.

"It's all right," Jake whispered in his wife's ear. "We've got plenty of time; there's no rush."

Yeah, right, Jake thought now. *No rush.*

Jake chugged the rest of his Coke. He crushed the can in his hand, whipped it in the garbage, and jumped back on the bike. It was time to go.

*

The Borderline looked deserted, but Jake took a chance anyway.

"So," Kevin asked Adrian as she dismounted the bike, "what did you think?"

"I hate to admit it," she grinned, "but you were right. It was awesome."

"Until…."

"Until?" she asked in confusion.

"You know what I'm talking about."

"Well, look at that," Adrian said after Maggie opened the front door. "Bar's open after all."

"Jake," Maggie said, her voice filled with compassion.

She stood in the doorway in her black sleeveless pantsuit and large gold hoop earrings, her arms stretched out to him.

"How you doing, hon?" she asked him as he stepped awkwardly into her warm embrace.

"I'm doing," Jake mumbled.

"Can't ask for more than that. Come on in. We've got our own little private party going on in here."

Maggie ushered Jake inside. Tony raised his glass to him from his seat at the far end of the bar.

"Go on; sit down," Maggie told him. "I was just about to get us another pitcher."

Jake noticed a third beer glass on the bar and wondered who else could've been there with them.

His question was answered when he heard the bathroom door shut. Cassie stopped cold when she saw him.

"Jake."

"Cass."

Maggie's eyes darted back and forth between the two of them. Jake seemed all right, but something was definitely up with Cassie.

"I…uh…was just telling Jake he should sit down and join us," Maggie stammered.

"You guys go ahead," Cassie replied. "I think I've reached my limit for tonight."

"No, please," Jake insisted. "Stay."

"Really?"

"Really."

"All right," Cassie eventually agreed.

"Great," Maggie responded, a little too enthusiastically.

Oh, my God; oh, my God; oh, my God, Cassie thought as she made her way to the bar. *I couldn't even make it through the funeral, but now I'm supposed to sit here and drink with Jake! This is insane!*

"No, it's not," Adrian told her. "You guys are friends. He doesn't blame you. You need to stop blaming yourself. It was just my time to go; that's all."

"Hmm," Kevin said as he came up behind her. "I think I've heard that somewhere before."

"I already said you were right once tonight," Adrian replied. "Let's not push it."

"I'm just saying."

"All right, everybody," Maggie said as she set the pitcher down on the bar, "come and get it while it's still cold."

They all sat around the bar and stared mournfully into their full glasses of beer. Nobody said a word.

Adrian saw the wheels turning in Maggie's mind, but Maggie took one look at each of them and just plopped down onto her stool.

"Wow," Kevin said sarcastically, "your friends really know how to have a good time, don't they?"

Adrian glared at him before she leaned over the bar by Maggie.

"C'mon, Maggie," Adrian said to her. "Don't give up so easily. You always know what to do to break us out of our moods. You've never let me down before. Please don't start now."

Maggie slammed her hand down on the bar and shocked all of them back to their senses.

"All right, that's it!" she declared. "Enough of this shit. Adrian would not want us all sitting around here crying in our beer for her."

"That's right," Adrian said.

"So what should we be doing instead?" Tony asked.

"Celebrating her life," Maggie answered. "And I know just where to start."

A smile spread across Adrian's lips while she watched Maggie move decisively around the bar to the jukebox.

When she plugged it in, the room suddenly exploded with music before she could even insert any money.

Adrian jumped back; her smile vanished. She turned to Kevin, who stood alongside the jukebox, and narrowed her eyes at him.

"'Folsom Prison Blues'! Really?"

"What?" Kevin feigned innocence while he raised his palms up helplessly to her.

Cassie couldn't resist. "Yeah, because nothing says Adrian Riley like a classic Johnny Cash song."

Everyone laughed.

"If she were here right now," Jake added, "she'd be ripping that plug right out of the socket to make that 'country shit' stop."

"If only I could," Adrian groaned.

"So why did you play it?" Tony asked Maggie.

"I didn't; I swear. It just came on."

Adrian shot Kevin a dirty look.

"Must've just been left over from last night or something," said Maggie, shrugging. "Who knows?"

"Oh, I do," Adrian said.

"Hey, I have no control over what someone else played on this jukebox last night," Kevin tried to defend himself. "But it did lighten the mood, didn't it?"

Adrian looked at each of them. The tension had eased from their faces.

"Not the point," she grumbled.

Maggie dug into her pocket for some change, inserted it, and made a new selection. "Now this is Adrian's song."

"There we go," Adrian said as she closed her eyes and swayed back and forth to "In the Air Tonight."

"Especially after she had a few drinks in her," Cassie added fondly.

Jake's mind flashed back to the night they had met.

I was afraid I was going to have to settle for the Kardashian wannabes, but then she came back.

And I caught her looking at me, not with disgust but a little bit of— what?—disappointment, maybe in her eyes.

That's when I knew. I had gotten to her, just like she had gotten to me that morning.

Adrian's mouth fell open after she heard her husband's revelation.

"You mean I wasn't just another hot girl in a car to him?"

Kevin laughed. "No, you weren't."

I couldn't tell her that, though, Jake continued. *I mean, what kind of man would admit that to any woman? What I did say instead did sound like a really good pick-up line, but it wasn't. It was the honest-to-God truth. And it worked.*

She finally let me buy her a drink, and we were on our second one when her favorite song came on. Over and over again.

That night, Jake had asked Adrian, "Is the jukebox broke or something?"

"I don't think so. Why?" she asked.

"Because it keeps playing this same stupid song."

"It's not stupid."

Jake gauged her reaction. "Oh no? You did that, didn't you?"

"Yep," Adrian replied proudly while she took a swig of beer.

"Why?"

"Why? Why not? It's the best drum solo in any song that's ever been played. Ever." She slammed her beer bottle down for emphasis.

"Oh, I wouldn't go that far."

"I would," Adrian said with a confident grin. "And I believe I just did."

"Yeah, you did, didn't you? Now you know you just can't toss out a statement like that without anything to back it up with. So c'mon; tell me what makes that song the best that's ever been played?"

"Well," Adrian began. She was at a complete loss for words until Cassie swooped in behind her.

"Because her dad plays the hell out of that song, that's why!"

"Yeah, that's right."

"Ah," Jake teased her, "so you're a daddy's girl, huh?"

"No, that's not it at all. You'd have to see my dad play it to understand."

"So your dad's a musician?"

"He's the drummer for The Uprising."

Adrian waited for the realization to hit, but it never came. Jake just stared blankly at her.

"Oh, c'mon! You can't tell me you live around here and you've never heard of The Uprising before?"

"Nope. Can't say that I have."

"Why am I talking to you again?"

"Because I obviously need to be enlightened."

"Yes, you do."

Adrian leaned in close to Jake, inches away from his lips, before she turned away.

"Hey, Maggie," she yelled, "when's the next time The Uprising's playing here?"

"Not till next Saturday night. Why?"

"What do you say?" Adrian locked eyes with Jake once more.

"To what?" Jake asked.

"You. Me. Here. Next Saturday night?"

"What? Like a date?"

"Well," she responded with a mischievous smile, "somebody's got to enlighten you."

"Jake?" Maggie's voice suddenly sliced through his memories. "You okay? You need anything?"

He suddenly felt the heat from their concerned eyes upon him. The song had long since ended; an eerie silence threatened once more.

"Just for you to play it again, please."

Maggie grinned. "Honey, I'll play it all night long if you want me to."

And so it went. They spent the rest of the night eating, drinking, and sharing their best Adrian stories until Cassie glanced at the neon blue clock behind the bar.

"Holy shit," she said. "It's that time already?"

"What's the matter?" Jake teased. "You going to turn into a pumpkin if you stay out too late or something?"

"No," Cassie replied. "I just have to be up early tomorrow."

"Early?" Jake asked. "For what?"

"My first therapy session," Cassie mumbled.

"Therapy?" Maggie asked.

"Yeah. It's a mandatory thing. I have to be cleared by a psychiatrist before they'll let me go back to work."

"Oh, please," Jake replied scornfully. "I'd rather quit my job than go talk to a shrink."

"Well, of course," Adrian said, her voice heavy with sarcasm, "because sharing your feelings is the last thing any man would want to do."

Cassie's face fell. "Yeah, well, what can I say? I love what I do so…." She responded with a shrug of her shoulders.

"I suppose. I better hit the road. Goodnight, guys, and thanks again," she said to Maggie and Tony as she stood up and swung her purse over her shoulder.

"'Night Cass," they both responded.

She headed for the door without so much as a glance back in Jake's direction. He remained on his stool and concentrated on removing a spot off his beer glass with his thumbs.

Maggie, Tony, and Adrian all stared daggers at him.

"What the hell?" Adrian yelled at her husband. "Don't just sit there like a dumb-ass! You know you screwed up. Now man up and do something about it already! Go on. GO…ON…!"

Adrian kept needling him until his conscience couldn't take anymore.

"Hey, Cass, wait up!" Jake said as he finally jumped off his stool. "Let me walk you out."

She turned around, frustration written all over her face. "You don't have to do that," she told him.

"Yeah, actually, I think I do."

She sighed as she motioned for him to lead the way outside.

They stood on the sidewalk underneath the streetlight. Cassie stared absentmindedly at the traffic that sped past them, her arms crossed in front of her. Jake stared down at his shoes, his hands thrust deep into his pockets.

Adrian looked at Kevin in disbelief.

"This is ridiculous," she said to him. "He's a grown man, not a kindergartner on a playground."

"You do realize we are talking about Jake here, right?" Kevin replied.

Adrian groaned.

"So," Cassie muttered.

"So," Jake repeated while he rocked on his heels.

Adrian leaned forward. She expected to hear more, but he never elaborated.

"C'mon, Jake," Adrian pleaded with him. "It's not that hard. Just say it already."

"Cass," Jake spoke tentatively after he pried his eyes away from his shoes and onto her.

"Yeah?"

"I…uh…I'm…sorry if I upset you in there with that shrink comment."

Cassie stared at him, her eyebrows raised in shock. "Wow," she said. "Look at that. Your first breakthrough. And I'm not even a licensed psychiatrist," she teased him.

"Shut up!"

"C'mon; you've got to admit you deserved that."

"Yeah, I guess so," Jake laughed. "So," his voice trailed off while he motioned back and forth between the two of them with his index finger, "you and me? We're all good now?"

Cassie chuckled. "Yeah, we're good."

"Okay. Good."

"Goodnight, Jake," she said as she leaned in to give him a hug. "And if you ever need to have another therapy session, you just give me a call, okay?"

"We'll see about that," Jake joked.

Adrian was fine when they hugged. What got to her was what happened next.

Cassie backed away slowly. She smiled affectionately at Jake. He watched her go. She should've turned around; he could've looked away, but they didn't. Their eyes remained locked onto each other a little longer than Adrian would've liked.

An ugly feeling suddenly overcame Adrian. Her stomach twisted and churned. Tiny sparks of irritation fueled an uncontrollable rage inside of her. The next thing she knew, the bulb in the streetlight above Cassie and Jake hissed and popped before it burnt out completely.

"Holy shit!" Cassie shrieked. "What was that?"

"Must've been a power surge or something," Jake answered as he glanced up at the light. "And now we're in the dark."

"I think that means it's time to head home."

"Yeah, I think maybe you're right. I'll talk to you later."

"Later."

Kevin narrowed his eyes at Adrian.

"What?" Adrian asked defensively. "What are you giving me that look for?"

"Because," Kevin replied, "it looks to me like Jake's not the only one who has some jealousy issues."

"What are you talking about? I've never been jealous a day in my life."

"Well, there's a first time for everything. That light bulb didn't just explode on its own, Adrian."

"So what? You think I got so jealous of Cassie and Jake that I made that light bulb explode?"

"I don't think; I know just by looking at you."

Adrian stared at Kevin in confusion. He motioned for her to turn around so she could take a look at her reflection through the plate glass window of The Borderline.

Adrian's jaw dropped. The outline of her body had a bright green glow to it.

"That bad feeling you just had in the pit of your stomach," Kevin told her.

"Yeah?" Adrian answered nervously.

"That's jealousy. And you're going to have to do a lot better job of controlling it if you want to help Jake."

*

Jake fell onto the couch and stared blankly ahead of him at nothing. All he could think about was the way he and Cassie had looked at each other before they left.

"See?" Adrian immediately exclaimed. "I can't believe it! I had every right to be jealous!"

"Whoa! Easy there, kiddo. You're getting all lit up again," Kevin told her.

He was right. Adrian saw the green light glowing brighter around her through the blank television screen in the living room. She took a deep breath to try to calm herself.

"Sorry," she muttered.

"It's all right," Kevin replied. "It's easy to jump to conclusions, but you really should wait until you hear everything first."

They both turned back to Jake, whose mind was still racing.

Cassie didn't look at me the way everyone else did. There was understanding there, not pity, like she knew exactly what I was going through.

And maybe she does. I mean, she was there when Adrian died too. I lost my wife and she lost her best friend.

Adrian felt her cheeks burn. She stared down at the floor to avoid facing Kevin. She felt bad enough as it was; she didn't need to see the disappointment in his eyes too.

"I'm not disappointed in you," Kevin said to her. "I just want you to try to think before you react next time; that's all."

Adrian sighed as she glanced over at her husband. She knew that was going to be easier said than done.

Chapter Thirteen

The days grew shorter, the air colder. Summer quickly faded into fall, just as Adrian's death faded into the back of most people's minds. Yes, it was a terrible tragedy, but life went on. Unfortunately, it wasn't that simple for Jake.

The days all blended together, one right into the next. Nothing really mattered to him anymore. He was just going through the motions, and he hid it so well that no one would've guessed. No one, that is, except for Adrian.

Adrian didn't need the added insight she had suddenly been blessed with to see through her husband. This charade was eating at him, and it was agonizing for her to watch day after day.

Jake woke up every morning well before his alarm clock went off. His first thoughts were always of her, but he never allowed them to linger too long. He made sure to shove them as far back into the recesses of his mind as he could before his feet even hit the floor.

Then there was work. Jake showed up with the same attitude he'd always had. None of the guys on his crew were the get-in-touch-with-their-feelings types. They'd ask him how he was doing; he'd give the same vague answer: "I'm doing," which was good enough for them.

When quitting time came, he'd go out with the guys for a drink or two like usual. Adrian noticed that Jake milked those few drinks like there was no tomorrow. He was usually one of the last ones to leave. He never really seemed to be in a hurry to get home.

Jake would jog up the stairs, but inwardly, he felt as if he were carrying the weight of the world on his back. He braced himself for the sucker punch that came whenever he opened the front door to his empty apartment.

Every once in a while, he'd think about finding someplace new to live, but that was all it was—just a passing thought. He couldn't. Not yet, anyway. It just didn't feel right to him.

So Jake would come inside to find supper waiting for him on the kitchen counter. He had given his mother a spare key when they first moved in, just for emergencies. She used it now to drop off food from the pizzeria for him every night, but he barely had an appetite anymore. No matter what it was—deep-dish pizza, stuffed crust, even their homemade twisted garlic breadsticks—he wouldn't touch it. The food took up space on the counter, just more leftovers for Jake to donate to the guys at work. Why give his mother anything to worry about when she came over the next night?

After that, he'd flop onto the couch in the living room and stare at whatever was on TV until his eyelids grew heavy and sleep overwhelmed him.

Wash. Rinse. Repeat.

And so it went. Life wasn't getting any harder or easier for Jake. It just was.

"All right, that's it!" Adrian leapt from her rocking chair one night after Jake came home. "I'm done!"

Kevin sat back on the recliner and watched her sudden outburst with interest.

"Can't we go see someone else," Adrian demanded. "Cassie…Laura… hell, *my parents* even?"

"Nope, sorry," Kevin replied.

"Why not? Why do we have to keep sitting here just…watching him fall apart?" Adrian's voice cracked at the end of her rant.

"Because," Kevin explained, "I've been waiting for you to get pissed off enough to do something."

"Do something?" she asked incredulously. "Like what?"

"I don't know. Take him by the hand…get him off this stupid hide-a-bed…lead him through a doorway maybe. You tell me. It doesn't have to be anything spectacular. Just do something so he'll at least try to get over that first hurdle."

Adrian was just about to defend herself when she stopped. Kevin was right. What exactly had she been doing other than standing around and watching her husband? This was all up to her. She couldn't rely on anyone else. Yes, Kevin was there to help her, but not to do everything for her.

"All right," she conceded.

"Good. It's about time."

Adrian let that comment slide. "I have an idea, but I don't even know if it's possible."

Kevin laughed. "Anything's possible now."

"Even Jake seeing me as if I were still alive?"

"Sure."

"And not freaking out about it?"

Kevin stared at her as if the answer should be obvious. "What do you think dreams are for?"

"Sleeping." The word stumbled slowly off her tongue.

"Ah, you still have so much to learn."

"Such as?"

"Let's start by setting the mood of this dream of yours."

"To what?"

"That is entirely up to you."

"Great," Adrian groaned.

It didn't take as long as she thought to come up with the perfect idea.

"Got it," she said with a knowing smile.

"Good, then I'll leave you to it."

And just like that, Kevin had disappeared. Adrian's eyes roamed frantically around the room.

"Kevin? Where'd you go?"

"I'm giving you and your husband some privacy," he answered. "Don't worry; you got this."

"I got this." She didn't sound as convinced as Kevin.

Adrian approached the couch where Jake lay, his head slumped over to the side, his eyes inches away from closing. By the time she reached him, her outfit had changed to the oversized Cubs T-shirt she normally wore to bed.

"What the…?"

"We have to make it look realistic," Kevin told her.

Okay.

Next, she needed to adjust the television set. There was some *Law & Order*-type show on. Adrian wasn't quite sure how to do it, so she just used the trial and error method.

She snapped her fingers, recited magic words. She even tried mental telepathy, but nothing worked until she waved her hand in front of the screen in defeat.

Crackling, gray static suddenly devoured the clear picture. Adrian stared at the set in amazement.

"Really? That's all it takes?"

Jake began to stir. Adrian turned toward him nervously and waited for his reaction.

Oh, God, please let this work.

"Hey, sweet thing," he said groggily while he stretched his arms out over his head.

He seemed fine, as if it were perfectly normal for her to be standing there. But Adrian was a basket case. Thankfully, Kevin was able to talk her through it.

"Just relax. Act natural."

Act natural, Adrian reminded herself before she attempted to speak to her husband.

"Hey," she eventually stammered.

Jake squinted while his eyes searched around the living room. "What time is it?" he asked.

Adrian felt her heart rate begin to slow. "Late enough," she answered, motioning with her head toward the television.

Jake sat up and saw the static on the screen. He looked sheepishly at Adrian. "Oh, man, I fell asleep out here again, didn't I?"

"Mm-hmm."

"I'm sorry," he said before letting out a huge yawn.

"It's all right," Adrian replied as she shut off the TV. "Just come to bed. I was starting to get pretty lonely in there without you."

She held her hand out expectantly to him. He gave her a mischievous grin.

"Well, we can't have that now, can we?"

"No," Adrian shook her head, "we cannot."

"I say it's time you take me to bed, Mrs. Riley."

He stood up and took Adrian's hand. She wasn't prepared for the way her husband's touch startled her.

"You all right?" he asked her.

Adrian waited for her heart to settle down. "Never better," she replied breathlessly as she led him slowly down the hall to their bedroom.

Jake followed her over the threshold. Adrian pulled him playfully to her; they tumbled onto the bed.

Jake pinned Adrian underneath him, one strong arm set firmly on either side of her. He couldn't take his eyes off his wife.

"What?" she asked uneasily.

"You are just so damn beautiful," he answered.

"Yeah, right."

"These lips," Jake said as his mouth hovered over hers, "would never lie about something like that."

Adrian never intended for it to go as far as it did, but she couldn't resist the sweet taste of his kiss or deny the ecstasy she felt while he massaged every inch of her with painstaking care.

She reveled in her husband's embrace for the rest of the night. His snoring in her ear sounded like a favorite song she hadn't heard in forever. Soon their eyes shut and they both drifted off to sleep with the exact same thought in their minds:

I wish we could stay like this forever.

*

Laura slammed the phone down in frustration. She had been trying to get ahold of her son since early this morning; it was almost noon now. He had promised to come down to the pizzeria first thing to help her out, but so far, he was a no-show. She had left messages everywhere for him: his cell phone, his home phone, but she had heard nothing back.

He always returned her calls, even if he got called in to work he still carried his cell phone on him and checked it frequently enough to know he should get back to her right away.

Something was wrong; Laura felt it. She couldn't wait any longer. She needed to get over there now.

Laura had never driven so fast before in her entire life. Her mind raced with all kinds of possibilities that ranged from the logical to pure paranoia. She didn't even remember the drive over to Jake's place. Laura was amazed she even got the key in the front door with the way her hands were shaking so badly.

"Jake!" she shouted hysterically.

She tore through the living room and into the kitchen where she found the pan of lasagna she had brought over the night before exactly where she had left it, untouched.

Laura's heart leapt into her throat.

Where is he? Why isn't he here? Why isn't he answering me?

"Jake! Jacob!" she screamed.

She continued her search, and stopped dead in her tracks in the doorway of Jake's bedroom.

"Oh, my God." Laura covered her mouth with her hand. "Jacob," she whispered.

She watched in awe as her son slept soundly in his own bed. He lay on his stomach on the right side of the bed; his left arm peeked out from underneath the blanket and rested gently on the pillow beside him.

Paranoia got the better of her once more.

What if he was sleeping too soundly?

Laura couldn't help herself. She snuck quietly into the room and hovered over her son until she saw the gentle rise and fall of his chest. She was about to pull back when Jake stretched out and opened his eyes.

He nearly jumped out of his skin when he saw his mother standing there.

"Jesus Christ, Mom!" he shouted. "You scared the hell out of me... again!"

Jake almost crushed Adrian, who instinctively drew her knees as well as the blanket up to her chin the second she saw her mother-in-law, even though she knew no one could see her. No one, that is, except for Kevin who had suddenly reappeared in the room behind Laura.

Laura blinked slowly, stunned by her son's reaction. "I'm sorry, but I've been looking everywhere for you." She paused so he wouldn't hear her voice break. "Believe me, this is the last place I expected to find you."

"Why?" Jake arched an eyebrow at his mother in confusion. "This is my bedroom."

"Exactly."

Jake rubbed the sleep from his eyes with his fists while the fog that clouded his mind slowly lifted.

The bedroom. She brought me in here last night after I fell asleep on the couch. She was right here beside me in my arms....

Reality bore down hard upon Jake.

It was just another damn dream.

He turned to the other side of the bed and was about to get up when he saw the wedding photograph Adrian kept on her nightstand.

Adrian set her feet on the floor, ready to run just in case Jake decided to bolt, but he didn't. He couldn't take his eyes off that picture.

That was, by far, the best day of my life, Jake thought to himself.

Adrian's lips curled up into an easy smile while she leaned into her husband.

"I got to admit," she said, "you did good, babe."

I told her she could do whatever she wanted for the wedding, so long as I could pick the first song we danced to.

"Which you kept from me right up until the music played!"

Jake smirked.

I escorted her out to the middle of the dance floor and made sure she kept her back to the stage so she couldn't see her dad sneak in behind the drum set. The look on her face when he started to play "In the Air Tonight" was priceless.

"I tried to look back at my dad, but you wanted my full attention while you circled around me, eyeing me up the same way you did when we first met."

I stopped in front of her, pulled her tight to me, and just waited for the drum solo to kick in.

"And that's when you dipped me. I was so not ready for that. I had to hang on to my veil for dear life."

Yeah, that was a good night.

But it's over now, just like your time with Adrian.

Jake bit down hard on his lip to fight the devastation he felt. He opened the drawer, stunned to find Adrian's camera inside it.

C'mon, man; snap the hell out of this, he scolded himself.

Now!

Jake tipped the picture over, face down, and placed it in the drawer before he made his way to the bathroom.

His head hung low while he gripped both sides of the sink. He couldn't bear to see his own reflection in the mirror.

Jake had never felt this kind of pain before.

C'mon, man; pull yourself together already!

I can't. It just hurts too damn much. Thank God no one else can see me like this right now.

Adrian slumped against the wall in front of her husband, her eyes filled with concern. She longed to do something—anything—for Jake.

She placed her fingers underneath his chin. Jake's head inched upward until it was level with the mirror. He looked like hell.

Adrian felt the anger building up inside of him.

That's the sorriest excuse for a man I've ever seen!

"God damn it!" Jake screamed before he slammed the palm of his hand into the mirror and shattered it. "Son-of-a-fucking bitch!"

Adrian ducked to avoid the falling shards of glass.

"Jake!"

Laura couldn't get to her son fast enough. Adrian was stunned to see her mother-in-law break down the locked door. Laura's wild eyes leapt from Jake to his bloodied hand.

All Laura could think about was a night not long after Kevin had died. There had been no down time for her after the funeral, nor did she want any. She jumped right back into managing the pizzeria and raising Jake, despite the protests from her family. They kept hounding her to take a night off for herself, but Laura always came up with some excuse why she couldn't. Then her brother Bobby informed her that he had managed to score tickets to a monster truck show at the arena downtown for him and Jake, which just happened to fall on a night she wasn't scheduled to work.

"We've got all the bases covered," Bobby told her.

"But…" Laura replied.

"No buts! Just go, relax, and enjoy yourself for one night for a change."

Laura had no choice now. So she bought takeout from a Chinese restaurant and settled in on the couch to watch *Mystic Pizza*. She got as far as the movie's opening credits.

There Laura was, eating her favorite food, watching her favorite movie, when the silence suddenly overwhelmed her. She was alone. Kevin wouldn't be hovering over her shoulder cracking jokes during the dialogue or stealing some of the fortune cookies away from her when she wasn't looking.

And he never would be again.

The container of shrimp fried rice tumbled onto the floor as Laura raced into the bathroom where she too faced her own reflection in the mirror. The only difference was that instead of smashing her hand against the glass, Laura grabbed a full bottle of sleeping pills from the medicine cabinet that her doctor had prescribed for her. She held it in her hand for the longest time and was seconds away from swallowing all of them when Bobby brought Jake back home.

Adrian turned to Kevin. Her eyes frantically searched his for any indication that this couldn't be true, but his face remained stoic.

"Jake doesn't know about this, does he?" she asked him.

"No," Kevin answered simply.

"Mom..." Jake began in exasperation, but his tone switched to concern once he actually looked at her and saw the panic in her eyes. "Mom?"

Laura wasn't listening. All she could think about was that awful night. The ache in the pit of her stomach that only got worse the more she thought about Kevin. How tempting it would have been just to drift off into one long, endless nap or, better yet, eternity with her husband.

She scrutinized her son to make sure he showed no signs of that same hopelessness.

Please, oh dear, God, please, don't let him be thinking that same thing.

Laura wasn't about to stand by and let that happen to Jake.

"You're getting help," she said.

It wasn't a request.

Chapter Fourteen

Jake slouched in his chair in the waiting room with his arms crossed and a grim expression on his face.

He hated this. Every single second of it. The last thing he wanted to do was pour his heart out to some stupid shrink he barely even knew. What would be the point, except to humiliate himself?

The point, Jake knew, was that this was what his mom wanted him to do. He glanced down at his bandaged hand.

Jesus!

Jake cringed every time he thought about her charging through that bathroom door. He'd never forget that look in her eyes. There was no way he could've refused anything she asked of him after that.

"Jake," the receptionist suddenly called out, "Dr. Kelly will see you now."

He stood up and trudged toward the doctor's office as if he were taking his first steps toward death row.

"C'mon," Kevin said to Adrian.

"This isn't going to be good, is it?" Adrian asked him as she rose reluctantly from her seat.

Kevin shrugged. "Only one way to find out."

They followed Jake inside the doctor's office. He came to a dead stop on the cream-colored carpeting.

It wasn't because of the spectacular view of the bay from the window, or the over-stuffed tan couch that stretched out alongside the doctor's desk. What really took him by surprise was the doctor herself.

She sat behind her desk, her face locked onto her computer. Her fingers moved rapidly over the keyboard, pausing only once to tuck a strand of her wavy blonde hair behind her ear.

"Whoa!" Jake thought to himself.

"What's he 'whoaing' about?" Adrian asked.

"Calm down," Kevin warned her. "You're starting to get a little green around the edges again."

"I can't help it!" Adrian admitted as she threw her hands up in the air. "I may be dead, but it still bothers me to see my husband eyeing up another woman."

Kevin put his hand up to his forehead. "Remember what I told you about jumping to conclusions?"

"Yes, but I don't think I jumped this time."

"Well, we'll see."

"Dr. Kelly?" Jake asked tentatively.

"Mm-hmm," the doctor responded, her eyes still intent on her computer screen.

"Dr. Jamie Kelly?"

The uncertainty in his voice caused her to quit typing. She turned slowly toward him.

"Yes," she replied.

Aw shit! Jake thought to himself. *This shrink's a woman…and hot as hell besides!*

Adrian glanced at Kevin with an I-told-you-so look on her face.

"Keep listening," he told her.

Dr. Kelly removed her glasses and stared thoughtfully at Jake.

"You weren't expecting someone else were you? Like a man maybe?"

"No," Jake responded as nonchalantly as he could.

"So you're okay with having a female therapist?"

His father's voice suddenly overtook his thoughts.

Never, ever, under any circumstances, let a woman know how you really feel. It makes you look weak in their eyes, and no woman likes a weak man.

"Whatever woman told you that was lying through her teeth," Adrian said to Kevin.

"No woman," Kevin replied. "That was just the advice my father gave me and his father gave him...."

"And so on and so on?"

"Yep."

"Unbelievable," Adrian muttered.

"Hey, I never thought Jake would apply it to a female psychiatrist. Then again," Kevin added, "I never thought he'd have to go see a psychiatrist."

"Jake?" Dr. Kelly suddenly interrupted his thoughts. "Are you all right?"

"Yeah, I'm fine."

It doesn't really matter anyway, Jake thought. *I wasn't planning on opening up to a guy, and I'm sure as hell not about to open up to a woman, hot or not.*

"Good. Why don't you have a seat and we'll get started."

Jake eyed the couch warily before he sat down on it. His body remained stiff even after the pile of decorative pillows fell into him like dominoes.

It was the longest hour of Jake's life. He felt like he was being interrogated. He revealed absolutely nothing to Dr. Kelly, no matter how hard she tried. When only five more minutes were left in the session, she again explained to Jake that this was a safe haven for him; he could tell her anything he wanted. She wouldn't pass judgment on him, and everything he said would stay strictly between him and her.

"Well, in that case," Jake said as he leaned forward and glanced at the clock on the wall to make sure their time was almost up, "I'll be perfectly honest with you. The only reason I'm here is because my mother wants me to be here. And I'm going to keep coming here until she thinks I'm better. But that doesn't mean I have to tell you anything, except for maybe this: I'm not a sensitive guy. I don't want to get in touch with my inner feelings. I'm just not wired that way. No offense, but there's nothing you can say or do that's going to change that.

"So, unless you've got another psychological trick up your sleeve you'd like to try, I think my hour's up."

"I think you're right," Dr. Kelly agreed. "I'll see you next week."

Jake got no farther than the elevator when his cell phone rang. He dug it out of the front pocket of his jeans, then rolled his eyes once he saw who it was.

"You just couldn't wait, could you?" he asked her.

"Hey, you should be glad I didn't ask to come sit in on your session with you," Laura replied.

"I'm surprised you didn't."

"So, c'mon. Tell me. How'd it go?"

"Great. Wonderful. I had an amazing breakthrough. She told me I'm cured and that I never have to come back again," he answered sarcastically.

"All right, smartass," she teased him. "That's enough now."

"What, Mom? Isn't that what you wanted to hear?"

"No," she answered through gritted teeth. "I wanted to know how it went."

"It went," he shrugged as the elevator doors opened and everyone spilled out into the lobby, "just like I thought it would. Except," he added while he lowered his voice, "that you forgot to tell me the doctor was a woman."

"I didn't forget. You just weren't listening to me. And even if I did, what's the big deal?"

Jake tipped his head back and shut his eyes. What was he thinking? He should've known better than even to bring up this subject to his mom. She was up on her soapbox now, ranting and raving about how men and women should be treated equally. God only knew how long she'd be up there for.

He considered hanging up on her, but that would've only pissed her off even more. So he continued on through the lobby with his cell phone inches away from his ear, "mm-hmming" and "yes-Momming" whenever he felt it was appropriate.

Meanwhile, Kevin and Adrian were outside in the parking lot. Adrian couldn't help but notice the way Kevin kept straining his neck to see who was coming through the entrance.

"Are you expecting someone?" she asked him.

"Where is she?" he mumbled under his breath. "She should've been here by now. They're going to miss each other."

"She? She who?"

Her question was answered moments later when a familiar cherry red Grand Am sped into the lot. Kevin seemed to relax the second he saw it.

Adrian turned to him while her mouth fell open.

"Cassie?" she asked.

Kevin didn't answer her. He was too caught up in the scene unfolding in front of him.

Jake had just walked out the front door, still trapped on the phone with his mother. His eyes roamed around everywhere except toward the back forty of the lot where Cassie had found the first available parking space.

"C'mon, Jake," Kevin urged him on. "Just look her way."

Adrian's eyes flashed with anger. "So what now? You want the two of them together, or was that your plan all along?"

Kevin sighed. "He needs her, Adrian."

"I thought he needed me!" Adrian snickered. "Now my husband needs my best friend too? For what?"

Kevin's eyes darted between Cassie, who was getting out of her car, and Jake, who was rapidly approaching his truck.

They're too far apart. They're going to miss each other.

Kevin needed to think of something fast.

"I don't have time to explain it to you right now," he said to Adrian. "So you're just going to have to trust me."

Adrian rolled her eyes. "Don't worry," she replied flatly, her voice laced with disgust. "He'll spot her."

"What? How?"

She shrugged. "Maybe you'll just have to trust me."

Kevin shot her a dirty look.

"The car alarm."

"What?" Kevin asked.

"The Grand Am is new. She's not used to locking the car with her keypad yet. Every time she tries, she hits the car alarm instead. Guaranteed."

They watched Cassie sprint about halfway down the aisle before she suddenly stopped.

Shit, she thought to herself. *I forgot to lock the doors.*

Sure enough, she spun around, aimed her key ring at her car, pushed down on the closest button, and set off the car alarm.

"Jesus!" Cassie shouted while she desperately attempted to silence the annoying sound. "Will you shut up already?"

"See," Adrian said to Kevin. "Told you. Now you can continue on with your matchmaking."

He tipped his head back and groaned. "I am not matchmaking."

Kevin ran his hand over his face before he locked eyes with Adrian.

"Just try to follow me here okay. Think about all of his friends, his family. My God, even you. Can you think of anyone he's ever felt comfortable enough around to really open up to about anything?"

Adrian thought it over. "Well, no, I guess not."

"So what do you think Dr. Kelly's chances are with him?" Kevin asked.

"If the sessions keep going as well as this one did? Probably slim to none."

"Exactly. So we need to keep searching for that one right person."

"And you think that's Cassie?" asked Adrian.

"I don't know," he replied. Adrian tilted her head and arched an eyebrow at him. "Honestly, I really don't. All we can do is give him the opportunity. The rest is up to him."

"So he could still ignore the car alarm, get into his truck, and just drive away?"

"If that's what he chooses to do. Yeah. Free will, remember? We can't make Jake do anything."

Adrian nodded while she studied her fingernails.

She looked up just in time to see Jake standing beside his open driver's side door. His head turned instinctively toward the wailing car alarm. It took him a minute before he recognized Cassie as the woman who was having the meltdown in the center aisle. He couldn't help but smile.

"Mom," he suddenly cut her off, "I'm going to have to let you go. There's someone here I need to help out."

"Oh, okay," she replied, surprised. "You are still coming down to the pizzeria tonight, right?"

Jake rolled his eyes. "Yeah, I guess so. I'll be there as soon as I'm done here."

He hung up his phone and strolled over to Cassie. She was still swearing up a storm when he reached her.

"You know," he told her, "it might work better if you started talking nicer to it."

Cassie jumped when she heard his voice. "Jake! What are you doing here?"

"Trying to keep you from getting arrested. May I?" he motioned to her keys.

"Have at it," she answered as she handed them over to him.

Jake kept his eyes on her while he pointed the key pad at her car and instantly silenced the obnoxious sound.

"Show off," she teased him.

He shrugged. "Years of practice with Adrian's Saturn."

The mention of Adrian's name struck them both silent.

"So," Cassie attempted to restart the conversation, "really. What are you doing here?"

"I…uh…had an appointment."

"Ah." A sly smile spread across Cassie's face. "So you finally caved in and went to see a therapist."

"I did not cave in. I was forced to go." *Oh yeah, that sounds much better.*

She wrinkled her eyebrows in confusion. "By who? Work?"

"No, someone much more powerful—my mom."

Cassie laughed. "Yeah, moms are kind of tough to cross."

"Yeah, I learned that one the hard way when I was younger. Never again. Which is why," he paused to glance down at his watch, "I agreed to meet her at the pizzeria for dinner right after my appointment."

"I need to get a move on too. I'm running late for my appointment."

They were just about to part ways when Jake suddenly spoke up. "Why don't you come with me?"

Cassie whirled around in surprise. "What?"

"What?" Adrian shrieked. "Did you put that idea in his head?" she asked Kevin.

"Nope, it was all his."

Yeah, what the hell? Jake thought. *Why not?*

"Come with me," he repeated, "to the pizzeria."

"Now?" Cassie replied.

"Why not?"

"What part of 'I'm running late for my appointment' didn't you understand?"

"Skip it," he answered with a careless shrug.

"I can't just skip it."

"Why not? You're already late anyway. C'mon; how could you possibly say no to a Mama Jo's pizza?"

"Oh, my God," Adrian said when Cassie didn't respond right away. "She's seriously considering it."

"And even if I did agree to do this, what would I tell my doctor?"

"Easy." Jake grinned as he pressed the button on her keypad and started up the alarm again. "Car problems. Remember?"

*

Jake swore his mother must've had some sort of tracking device implanted in him at birth because no matter where she was in the pizzeria or how crazy-busy it was, she always knew exactly when he came in.

Like tonight for example. The place was jam-packed with people, and the jukebox was blaring. Laura was underneath the bar, tinkering around with a plugged-up beer tapper. Nevertheless, she leapt to her feet the second her son walked through the front door.

"Finally!" Laura shouted as she tossed a bar towel over her shoulder and made her way toward Jake. "I was afraid we were going to have to eat in the kitchen if you didn't show up soon."

"Sorry," Jake said while he let his mother drag him by the hand through the restaurant, "but I...uh...ran into someone after my appointment."

"I kept telling everyone not to give this table away," Laura rambled on as if Jake hadn't spoken. "It's reserved for you and me."

"And one more."

"No exceptions. I didn't care if the pope himself walked in...."

"Mom."

"But I swear, Jake, if you would've shown up any later, I wouldn't have had a choice!"

"Mom!"

The sharpness in Jake's voice caused Laura to stop in her tracks.

"What?" she asked as she turned slowly around to face him.

"I hope you don't mind," he replied, "but I invited someone else to join us for dinner."

Laura blinked in confusion.

"Someone else?"

That's when she looked over her son's shoulder and zeroed in on Cassie.

"Hey, Mrs. Riley," Cassie said with an awkward wave of her hand.

"Oh. Hey, Cass."

Laura shot her son a not-so-subtle look.

"Our table's right over there in the corner." Laura put her hand lightly on Cassie's shoulder while she pointed her in the right direction. "So if you want to go grab a seat while Jake and I go get the food."

"Sure," Cassie said.

Jake couldn't help but smirk while he followed his mother back to the kitchen.

"So this is how you're going to play this, huh?" Laura asked him while she slid their pizza out of the warming oven.

"What?" he asked, playing innocent.

"Oh, don't you 'what' me," she said with a shake of her head. "Dragging poor Cassie down here just so you wouldn't have to talk to me about your therapy session."

That better be the only reason he invited her, Adrian thought.

Adrian suddenly felt Kevin's eyes boring into her. Her eyes fell guiltily onto the floor. She forgot her thoughts were no longer her own anymore.

"That's all right, though," Laura continued on to Jake. "I'll let you slide this time, but you know what that means, right?"

"What?"

"I'll have to get on you twice as bad next week."

"Well," Jake countered with a mischievous grin, "I guess that means I'll just have to keep bringing Cassie with me."

And with that, Jake snatched up their pizza in both hands and rushed out the kitchen door, just as Laura flung the bar towel at his head.

"He's just messing with her, right?" Adrian asked Kevin. "Please tell me he's just messing with her."

Kevin didn't answer.

Chapter Fifteen

"So what do you think?" Jake asked Cassie. "You up for doing this again next week?"

"I can't believe he's doing this," Adrian said while she rubbed her fingers across her forehead.

They were standing beside their vehicles outside of Mama Jo's. Jake's question caught Cassie completely off guard.

"Wait. What?" Cassie stammered.

"You heard me," Jake chuckled. "You had a good time tonight, right?"

"Yeah."

"So why not do it again?"

"Because you're my husband, that's why!" Adrian shouted without thinking.

"You'd actually be doing me a favor," Jake pressed on.

"Oh, really? How so?"

"Because everyone keeps telling me I need to get out more."

"Don't do it…. Don't do it…. Don't do it…." Adrian kept chanting to her friend until she finally answered Jake.

"Aw, what the hell."

"No," Adrian moaned, her head hung low with disappointment. She looked to Kevin. "Didn't she hear that nagging voice in her head telling her not to do it?"

"Yes, but she does still have a mind of her own," Kevin explained. "C'mon; you can't tell me you always listened to your voice."

"Well, no," Adrian admitted reluctantly, "but I also remember getting into a lot more trouble that way."

*

Jake leaned back against the front door, tossed his keys effortlessly into the bowl, then let out a long, slow breath before a look of contentment spread across his face.

Adrian suddenly felt a twinge of guilt in the pit of her stomach.

"I haven't seen him this relaxed since before I died," she admitted remorsefully.

Jake intended to crash on the couch and get lost in a little TV, until he noticed the blinking red light on the answering machine.

He stared apprehensively at it as if it were a detonator to a bomb.

Jesus Christ, not another condolence call.

Those were the only messages anyone ever left on there anymore since Adrian had died. Jake knew everyone meant well, but he could only take so much after a while.

His mother screened all the calls for him after he threatened to throw the machine off the balcony. This was the first one that had slipped by her.

He clenched his fists, his jaw set firmly. Every muscle in his body seized with tension as he instinctively went into his Riley stance.

"I don't get it," Adrian said to Kevin. "Why is this upsetting him so much?"

"It's not just the message," Kevin explained to her, "but the memories it brings up for him."

All Jake could think about was the day Adrian recorded their greeting.

They had just finished moving all of their stuff into the apartment. There were boxes stacked everywhere. They had no idea where anything was or where it needed to go. They were both so worn out and exhausted. Jake was ready to order a pizza and call it a day, but Adrian wouldn't give in until she dug out their new answering machine. He would've been perfectly happy to keep the bland, generic automated voice on there, but she insisted they make it personal.

He could still see her standing right there in the living room with her back to him in her gray Old Navy T-shirt and black nylon workout pants. She pulled her hair back in a ponytail as she leaned in close to the answering machine and tried to record a suitable message, but it wasn't working.

Jake sat on the couch with his feet propped up on a couple of cardboard boxes and watched his new wife with amusement. Adrian pressed her fingertips to her forehead and groaned in frustration. She turned around to see her husband laughing at her.

"Having a little trouble with this, are you?" Jake teased her.

"Yes, and it's all your fault!" Adrian answered good-naturedly.

"Me? What did I do? I'm just sitting here."

"You're making me very self-conscious."

"You, self-conscious?" Jake said as he stood up and made his way over to her. "You've never been self-conscious a day in your life."

"Yeah, well, I am now."

"Would you like me to leave the room?" he asked after he wrapped his arms around her waist and began to nibble on her neck.

"No, no. I think I've got it now."

"Wow," Adrian said in astonishment, "I can't believe he actually remembered all that."

"It must've really meant something to him," Kevin replied.

Jake groaned as he tipped his head back and shut his eyes.

Should I even bother playing it? If anyone really needed to get ahold of me—like mom or work—they would've tried calling my cell phone, right? It was probably nothing important. But what if it was?

Jake stared at the blinking red light.

"Looking at it is not going to make it stop," Kevin told him. "There's only one way to do that, so just be a man and hit the damn button already!"

Jake was just about to do that when the telephone rang.

The unexpected sound made him jump. He should've picked it up, but he couldn't. He just stood there, frozen in place, waiting for the machine to kick in.

"Hi, you've reached Adrian and Jake Riley." Adrian's voice oozed with happiness. "We can't make it to the phone right now, but if you leave a message, we'll get back to you as soon as we can."

"Oh, my God," Adrian gasped. "He still hasn't changed it."

"Nope," Kevin replied.

The sound of his wife's voice literally knocked Jake's legs out from underneath him. He dropped down onto the arm of the couch and stared at the machine for the longest time.

"Adrian?" Kevin asked her gently.

"Huh?"

"You still with me?"

That's when she realized she had fallen into the same trance that Jake had.

"Oh. Yeah. Sorry."

Nothing else registered for Jake after he heard Adrian's voice, not even the message. He was tempted just to walk away and forget about it, but something told him he needed to listen to it, so he pressed the play button again.

"Hi, Jake," the woman began tentatively. "It's Sam. Could you please call me back as soon as you get this? It's…um…kind of important."

Samantha Lancaster was Adrian's boss and, according to Adrian, a huge deal in the world of photography. Adrian had gotten a job interning with her while she was in college. Adrian had impressed Sam so much that Sam had offered her a full-time job after she graduated. Her official title was photographer's assistant, which basically meant she got to do everything no one else wanted to do, but Adrian didn't care. She was learning from the master, and she couldn't have asked for anything more.

"Call her back! Call her back! Call her back!" Adrian shouted frantically.

"Calm down," Kevin told her. "Give the man a minute, will you?"

"Sorry. I guess I got a little overexcited. This is the first time Sam's ever called the house."

Jake's shoulders sagged while he reached for the phone. *Great,* he thought to himself. *Now what?*

"Samantha Lancaster Photography," a woman answered.

"Hey, Sam; it's Jake Riley."

Adrian wrinkled her brows when she heard the casualness in her husband's voice as if he were talking to an old friend instead of her boss.

"Jake," relief flooded through her voice. "Finally!"

"Sorry it took me so long to get back to you," he mumbled. "You said you had something important to talk to me about?"

"Yes." Sam paused, uncertain how to begin. "I…uh…think it's time to cash in on that favor you owe me, Jake."

"Favor?" Adrian exclaimed in disbelief. "What favor?"

"You wouldn't happen to be available for lunch tomorrow, would you?" Sam continued.

Lunch? Really? Jake thought. *Why can't she just tell me whatever it is over the phone?*

"Jake?" Sam asked. "Are you still there?"

"Yeah. Yeah, I'm here."

"So what do you say?"

I say I never should've listened to this answering machine, that's what I say.

"Sure," Jake sighed. "What did you have in mind?"

"Well, I planned on taking some pictures out at Kingston Beach tomorrow if the weather holds out. Would one o'clock work for you?"

"Sure."

"Great. You still have my cell phone number right, just in case anything changes?"

"Yep."

"He has her cell phone number?" Adrian asked. *Why?*

"Great. I'll see you then."

Great, Jake thought less than enthused.

*

What the hell is going on here? Jake thought to himself as he pulled into the parking lot.

There wasn't a space to be found. It didn't make any sense. He could understand if it were the middle of July, but it was October, for Christ's sake. Who goes to an amusement park in October?

He cruised up and down every single aisle. The list of better things he could've been doing at that moment grew longer with every lap he took.

"He's going to get pissed," Adrian said, "and just say the hell with it and take off."

"No, he won't," Kevin replied.

"How can you be so sure?"

"Because." His eyes cut to a dark blue minivan that had just backed out of a parking space. "A spot just opened up for him."

Jake made a beeline for the space. He pulled the keys out of the ignition and glanced through the windshield.

Jake slumped back in his seat. His lips parted; his mouth went dry at the sight of The Fury right in front of him.

The Fury was the main attraction at Kingston Beach. It was a monstrous, classic wooden roller coaster with hairpin turns and heart-stopping drops, all set alongside the bay.

Jake stared at it now in stunned silence, not because he was afraid of the roller coaster, but because it had slammed him with yet another memory of his wife.

Adrian sat between Jake and Kevin, her feet propped up on the dashboard of the truck.

"It was a perfect spring day," she began. "The first one of the year, if I remember correctly.

"You know," Adrian turned her attention to Kevin, "the kind of day where you're just itching to be outside?"

"Mmm-hmm," Kevin agreed.

"So I called Jake."

Adrian called me just as I was about to take the bike out for a ride.

"Wait? What?" Adrian whipped her head around toward her husband. "You never told me that!"

Go take a ride by myself or spend the day with Adrian? Yeah, it was pretty much a no-brainer. So I picked her up in front of her apartment building and asked her what she wanted to do.

She had this look on her face, and I knew right away I was in trouble.

"Well, I…uh…just happened to see in the paper that Kingston Beach opens up today."

"Yeah," Jake replied uneasily.

"So, I thought maybe we could go there and ride The Fury."

"What? You're kidding, right?"

"C'mon; it'll be fun!"

Jake stared at Adrian as if she were crazy.

"What's the matter?" she asked him. "You scared?"

"Scared? Me? No way!"

"Well, let's go."

The next thing Jake knew, he was standing at the end of a very long line to ride the roller coaster.

They must've waited at least an hour if not more. Jake spent most of that time concentrating on Adrian.

Her hand felt warm and clammy inside of mine, but she wouldn't let go, and I didn't want her to, even when this little boy in front of us started tugging on her shirttail.

He couldn't have been more than maybe nine or ten years old. Anyway, he asked her something, and once she answered him, he just kept firing more questions at her.

Anyone else might've just blown him off, but not Adrian. She wiped the sweat from her brow, knelt down, and talked to him like he was the most important person she had been around all day.

Once her new friend got on the ride, she stood up and bounced on the tips of her toes as the cars took off down the tracks.

"We're next!" she said to me, her eyes all lit up with excitement.

I shook my head and grinned at her.

"What?" she blushed.

I was going to say it then, but a carload of screaming people plunged down the track in front of us at that exact same moment. Adrian looked up to watch them zoom by, and when she turned back to me, I kissed her on the lips instead. I didn't get another chance until after we got off the roller coaster.

Adrian stared at her husband as if she had just gotten a glimpse inside J.D. Salinger's journals.

"So, what did you think?" Adrian asked me as we walked through the exit together.

"Marry me," I blurted out.

"Wow," Adrian laughed, "that coaster really did a number on you didn't it?"

I stopped and looked deep into her eyes.

My heart felt like it was going to jump right out of my chest, but it wasn't because of the roller coaster. This wasn't something I had planned. Far from it! It just felt like the right moment to do it.

"I'm serious," I replied while I took both her hands in mine. "Marry me."

"I was blown away," Adrian admitted to Kevin. "I mean, my mind was gone. I couldn't have put two words together even if I'd tried. But I somehow managed to come up with:

"This is crazy; you know that, right? I mean, we just got off a roller coaster for crying out loud!"

"I know."

"What about a ring? Don't we need to have a ring?"

"Don't worry about a ring. Just answer my question. Will you marry me?"

"Well, yeah, but—"

I held up my hand to interrupt her. "Is that a 'Yeah, I'll answer your question,' or a 'Yeah, I'll marry you'?"

The anticipation nearly killed me while I waited for her response. "Yes," she finally answered, "I'll marry you."

A knock on the driver's side window startled Jake back to reality.

A petite woman with straight blonde hair and big brown eyes that betrayed her intelligence stood beside his truck. Those eyes grew even rounder after Jake jumped in his seat.

"Sorry," she apologized after he rolled his window down. "I didn't mean to scare you."

"That's all right, Sam," Jake replied. "You just caught me daydreaming is all."

He stepped out of his truck and followed her across the park to the nearest concession stand.

"Why is this place so busy today?" he asked her after they ordered their food.

"It's the last weekend of the season," Sam explained as she dug some money out of the pocket of her jeans to pay the vendor. "The park always closes with a big Halloween bash."

"And they hire you to take pictures of it?" asked Jake, handing Sam her food and then taking his.

"No," Sam answered while she took a big bite out of her apple-topped elephant ear. "I volunteer to do this kind of stuff."

"Really?"

"Don't sound so surprised." She paused to wipe some of the sticky mess from her face. "Sometimes, the best pictures aren't the ones people pose for."

Jake chuckled. "Sounds like something Adrian would say."

Sam caught the wistful smile that flashed across his face.

"C'mon," she told him. "Let's go find a place to sit down."

An awkward silence followed while they carried their paper plates to an empty picnic table near the playground.

"So," Jake began while he unwrapped his cheeseburger from its foil, "what's this all about?"

"Adrian," Sam answered hesitantly.

"I figured as much," Jake replied as he set his sandwich off to the side.

"It's just that I've been thinking about her a lot lately; her photographs in particular. I can't stop looking at them. And every time I do, I always come back to the same conclusion."

"Which is what?"

Sam looked Jake right in the eye. "She had a real gift, Jake. A gift that I believe needs to be shared."

Adrian's eyes practically popped out of her head.

"I'm not imagining this, right?" she asked Kevin. "You heard her say the same thing I did?"

"Yep," Kevin answered.

"Whoa. Wow!"

"So," Jake asked Sam, "what did you have in mind?"

"Well," Sam leaned forward, "I'd like to use my upcoming show this spring to showcase some of Adrian's work."

Adrian's jaw dropped while the rest of her body froze.

"Adrian," Kevin asked her, his voice full of concern, "you okay?"

"No," she said while the corners of her mouth upturned into a smile. "My very own show? No fricking way!"

Kevin chuckled. "Yes, way."

"Oh, my God. Oh, my God!" Then another thought popped into Adrian's head. "He better say yes! This is the chance of a lifetime! If he won't let Sam do this—"

"I don't think that's Sam's main concern."

Jake responded immediately. "Well, yeah, definitely! Whatever you want to do, I'm behind you 100 percent."

"Good," Sam replied. "I'm glad to hear that because I am going to need your help."

Jake's eyebrows wrinkled in confusion. "You do realize I know absolutely nothing about photography, right?"

"Yes, but you do know a lot about Adrian." The wrinkles deepened. "Let me explain."

"Please do."

"Well," Sam began as she glanced down at her fidgeting fingers, "all I have are the pictures from the portfolio Adrian sent to me when she was applying for her internship."

"Oh, I see. So you want me to find more of her pictures for you?"

"I know it's a lot to ask, and if it's still too difficult for you, I'll understand."

Jake's mind immediately went to Adrian's closet. All he could see were all the photo albums that had been collecting dust in a bedroom he could barely even bring himself to step inside of.

Jake's stomach tightened. Just the thought of looking through all of Adrian's albums, facing all of those memories, seemed impossible. He wanted to tell Sam there was no way in hell he could do that right now, but his pride got the better of him.

"No, it's fine. I'll get you whatever you need."

"Are you sure? You don't have to give me an answer right now. Take some time to think about it."

"I don't need to think about it. Let's do it."

Chapter Sixteen

Jake sat on the edge of his bed and glared at the closed closet doors in front of him. He swiped the bottle of beer off the nightstand and chugged it down in several angry gulps, his thirst nowhere near quenched. Jake needed another one, but he also needed to open those damn doors.

What's the big deal? It's just a closet, for Christ's sake! So why have I been sitting here for so fucking long? What the hell am I so afraid of?

Nothing! Jake tossed the bottle on the bed and marched toward the closet. He grabbed hold of the handles, but he couldn't go any farther. The memories paralyzed him; they were his own personal form of kryptonite. He lowered his head and shut his eyes while the rage erupted from him.

"God-damn, son-of-a-bitch!" Jake shook the doors as if he intended to rip them off their hinges just as his cell phone rang.

"What?" he snarled when he answered.

"Lose the attitude right now, Jacob."

"Oh." Jake instantly dialed it down several notches. "Sorry, Mom."

"You should be. Where are you? Cassie and I are waiting here at the pizzeria for you."

Shit! Their weekly dinner.

"I'm on my way," he told her.

*

Cassie and Laura sat in the corner booth and watched incredulously while Jake twirled the spaghetti around his fork but never bothered to bring it up to his lips.

"What's wrong?" Laura asked him.

"Nothing. Why?"

"Because you're playing with your spaghetti instead of inhaling it like you usually do."

"I'm just not hungry; that's all."

"Mm-hmm," Laura responded skeptically. "So I suppose you never made it to your therapy session this week either?"

"No, Mom," Jake answered while his fork clanked loudly against his plate, "I did not."

"Oh, Jacob." Disappointment saturated his mother's words.

Cassie sunk into her seat, her arms folded in front of her as if she were trying to make herself invisible.

"This isn't good," Kevin told Adrian. "We need to stop this before it gets out of control."

"No problem," Adrian replied while her eyes wandered to the other end of the pizzeria. "I know exactly what to do."

Moments later, a young waitress approached their booth.

"Um, Laura," she began nervously, "I really hate to bother you but…uh…there's a Mrs. Maloney at table twenty-three who insists on speaking to you right away."

"Dear God, that woman!" Laura rolled her eyes. "I swear she's going to be the death of me yet."

Cassie inched forward after Laura left. "What was all that about?" she asked Jake.

Jake grinned. "Mrs. Maloney's been coming here ever since I can remember. She loves this place."

"Okay," Cassie sounded confused.

"She always gives my mother helpful suggestions about the pizzeria, and once she starts, it's very difficult to get her to stop." He chuckled. "She's a pain in the ass, but I got to say her timing couldn't have been better tonight."

"Yeah," Adrian said with a twinkle in her eye as she glanced over at Kevin, "it's a good thing Mrs. Maloney came up with that idea for the menus when she did, huh?"

Her proud smile never faded, even though Kevin didn't give her the compliment she was waiting for.

That's all right," she said. "No thanks necessary."

"So," Cassie began as she reached for her beer.

"So," Jake shrugged.

Don't do it, Cassie kept telling herself. *Just leave it be. But what else are we going to do? Just sit here and stare awkwardly at each other until his mother comes back and starts World War III?*

"Oh, for God's sake!" Adrian yelled at her friend. "Just ask him already!"

"You want to tell me what's wrong?" Cassie asked.

Jake stared at Cassie, his expression indecipherable.

Not really, but if I have to choose between you or my mom….

"I…uh…I saw Sam the other day."

Cassie's eyes widened. "Adrian's Sam?"

"Yep, that would be the one."

"What did she want?"

"She...uh...she wants to do a show this spring using some of Adrian's work."

"You're kidding? No way! That's great!" But Cassie's enthusiasm took a nose dive once she saw Jake's reaction. "That's not great?"

He held his beer bottle in both of his hands and stared intently at it. "It is; it's just that...."

The words got caught in Jake's throat, but his wife heard them loud and clear.

It's those damn stupid photographs. Jake's eyes met Cassie's. *But I can't tell you that.*

"Yes, you can!" Adrian elbowed Kevin in the ribs. "Tell him—tell him it won't make him any less of a man!"

"I can't," Kevin replied remorsefully, "because he'll never believe it coming from me."

Adrian sighed in frustration. Jake ran his hands over his face.

"I've got to go," he told Cassie.

Cassie sat speechless while Jake slid swiftly out of the booth.

"Tell my mom I'm sorry."

All Cassie could do was turn and watch as Jake walked away from her. Adrian was having none of it.

"Oh, no!" Adrian said defiantly to her husband. "You are not getting away that easily!"

She leapt out of the booth and positioned herself directly in front of him. Her hands lay flat against his shoulders, but his will was far stronger than she was. He barreled over her on his way to the front door.

"No!" Adrian yelled as she lay on her back on the floor.

She looked behind her and saw that Mrs. Maloney still had Laura cornered. Kevin stood beside Laura. He positioned her so that she turned toward the front door just as her son exited through it.

Cassie felt Laura's eyes zero in on her all the way across the room. They implored her to go after Jake.

"Damn it," Cassie muttered as she flung her napkin down on the table.

Jake was already gone by the time she got out to the parking lot.

"Great," Cassie grumbled. "Now how the hell am I supposed to figure out where he went?"

"Try the most obvious place first," Adrian told her.

Cassie pulled into Jake's driveway and was relieved to find his truck there.

"Thank God!" she said as she stepped out of her car. "I really wasn't in the mood to go on a wild goose chase tonight."

She sprinted up the stairs but then halted in front of the door.

What am I going to say to him?

"Who cares?" Adrian shouted. "Just get him to let you inside!"

Adrian grabbed her friend's arm. Cassie felt like her fist had a mind of its own as she rapped loudly against the door.

Jake's face fell when he saw her.

"Cass, please, go home."

"Sorry," Cassie replied as she thrust her arm out to keep him from shutting the door on her, "but I'm afraid I can't do that."

"Fine, suit yourself."

Jake turned his back on Cassie and left her standing dazed in the doorway.

"Well, don't just stand there," Adrian said as she nudged her friend forward. "Get inside!"

"Jake," Cassie called out timidly. She crossed reluctantly over the threshold and trailed a safe distance behind him into the bedroom. "I just want to know what's wrong."

"What's *wrong*?"

He wheeled around to face her, his bright blue eyes now as dark as storm clouds on the horizon.

"Maybe this wasn't such a hot idea after all," Adrian murmured.

Cassie took a step back while Kevin stood in front of his son.

"Do not," Kevin told him, "take this out on her."

Jake cast his eyes downward as if he had just been disciplined.

"That's what's wrong," he said again in a much more subdued tone as he motioned toward the closet.

Cassie followed his intense gaze while her own eyes squinted in confusion.

"So…what?" Cassie deadpanned. "You think Adrian had some skeletons lurking in there or something? Trust me; you don't have to worry. You're not going to find a *Fifty Shades of Grey* sex store hiding in there."

"Oh, God, Cass," Adrian groaned. "Just stop talking already."

Jake's silence struck Cassie harder than any punch he could've thrown at her.

Cassie winced. *I should've just quit while I was ahead.*

She was about to start apologizing when she heard it. Cassie thought she imagined it. Adrian's mouth fell open.

"Is that laughter coming from my husband?"

"Well, I'll be damned," Kevin said.

"How did she get him to do that?"

"She must have the magic touch."

"Yeah, she must."

The bitterness in Adrian's voice caused Kevin to arch an eyebrow at her.

"What?" Adrian asked.

"Nothing," Kevin answered with a shake of his head.

"I wish," Jake admitted to Cassie, "it was something as simple as that."

Cassie sat down on the bed beside him.

"So what is it, if you don't mind me asking?"

"You just don't give up, do you?"

"Apparently not."

Jake laughed again. "All right, you win. I'll tell you."

"What?" Adrian looked at Kevin. "Just like that?"

"All of Adrian's photo albums are in there," Jake said.

"Just like that," Kevin answered Adrian.

"Oh." Cassie's voice trailed off while her eyes fixated on the closet doors.

"What is this?" Adrian asked. "The Bermuda Triangle? Now it's sucked them both in!"

"It scares the shit out of you, doesn't it?" Cassie stared straight ahead of her. "Thinking about what's behind those doors. I know the feeling. I don't have a closet, but I do have a shoebox full of souvenirs I kept from some of the things Adrian and I did together."

"I didn't know that," Adrian said.

"I thought it would be fun to hang onto all of it and maybe show it to our kids someday or something." Cassie sniffed. "I wanted to throw that box away after she died, but I just couldn't. So I shoved it as far underneath my bed as I possibly could, and I haven't looked at it since."

They sat in amicable silence.

"But you know what Dr. Kelly told me?" Jake scoffed, but Cassie continued anyway. "Sometimes, it's best just to rip the Band-Aid right off."

Cassie slapped the palms of her hands on her knees before she stood up.

"What are you doing?" Jake asked.

Cassie flung the closet doors open without saying a word. She glanced back at him to gauge his reaction.

Jake sat with his chest out and his chin up. He looked as detached as a soldier standing guard.

She got chills just looking at him.

"Then again," Cassie said while her eyes darted from Jake back to the closet, "what do therapists know, right?"

She was about to shut the doors when he stopped her.

"No. Don't. Please."

Cassie turned anxiously to him. "You sure?"

"Positive."

"Okay."

Cassie stepped aside while Jake came forward. Adrian peeked over his shoulder.

It looked exactly the way she had left it, including....

"Oh, shit." Adrian covered her mouth.

A dark blue flannel shirt of Jake's lay among the photo albums that littered the floor.

What's this doing in here? Jake thought.

"I wore it that morning," Adrian explained. "I wanted to wash it so he wouldn't know I borrowed it, but I ran out of time and just tossed it in there. I forgot all about it."

Jake reached for the shirt. Adrian's scent still lingered on the fabric. He shut his eyes. Cassie put her hand on his shoulder. Her touch felt like a live wire to him.

"Jake, are you all right?" Cassie asked.

His eyes popped open. He went to throw the shirt back into the closet when he felt something inside the pocket.

Shit, Adrian thought. *He found it!*

Jake knew, without even having to unfold the piece of paper, exactly what it said. He balled it up inside his fist and whipped it onto the floor before he left the room.

Cassie reached discreetly down to pick up the note. She smoothed the paper out and rocked back on her heels when she read it.

Couldn't wait. You made me late. Love ya, sweet thing.

"That was the last note Jake ever left for me," Adrian said wistfully.

Cassie jumped and fell flat on her ass when Jake barged back into the room with a big black garbage bag in his hands.

"What are you going to do with that?" Cassie asked.

"Whoa," Adrian said while Jake headed straight for the closet. "She's about as visible to him right now as we are."

"Jake?" Cassie asked hesitantly.

Still nothing.

She watched in stunned silence as he ripped Adrian's clothes off their hangers and threw them into the trash.

"Jake no!" Adrian screamed. "Stop it right now!"

But her words fell on deaf ears. Adrian could no longer hear her thoughts inside her husband's mind.

She turned to Kevin, her face panic-stricken. "What's going on? Why can't he hear me?"

Kevin stared dismally at his son. "The darkness is blocking you out."

"So what do I do?" Kevin didn't answer her. "What the hell am I supposed to do now?"

Kevin looked at her. "Get through to someone else."

Adrian took the hint. She rushed over to Cassie and helped her get back up on her feet.

"No!" Cassie shouted as she clamped her hand down on Jake's arm. "Not like this!"

Jake's eyes locked onto Cassie's hand before they shot up to her face. The tension between them intensified while they glared at each other.

Adrian felt Cassie's nervous energy.

"Do not let him intimidate you," Adrian told her.

Cassie grew more confident after Adrian took her hand firmly in hers. They stood shoulder-to-shoulder against Jake in an epic stare down that ended as Adrian's jaw dropped.

"Am I seeing what I think I'm seeing?" she asked Kevin.

"Yes," he answered, his voice flooded with relief, "you are."

The darkness poured out of Jake like a river of thick, black tar that pooled around his feet and eventually evaporated. His arm fell to his side; Adrian's beloved Sammy Sosa jersey slipped through his fingers and fell onto the floor.

Cassie moved swiftly from the room. Jake flinched when he heard the front door click shut. He bent down to retrieve his wife's jersey and hung it reverently back up on its hanger.

I never should've come here tonight, Cassie thought as she bolted down the stairs.

Chapter Seventeen

"**D**ude, you seriously need to get laid."

Charlie stood on the edge of his living room with a full bottle of beer in each of his hands while he assessed his best friend.

Jake lay sprawled out on the couch in a pair of green sweatpants and his Aaron Rodgers' jersey. It was a Sunday afternoon. Charlie had invited Jake over to watch the game with him.

Jake stared at his friend in confusion.

"What?"

"You heard me," Charlie answered as he handed him his beer. "No offense, man, but you're a mess."

"What are you talking about?" Jake asked as he brushed some Cheetos off his chest.

"You're kidding, right?" Charlie motioned to the 55" flat screen TV that hung on the far wall. "It's Packers/Bears Sunday and you're sitting here like we're watching a PBS special!"

Jake shrugged. "It's just not that exciting a game."

"It's Packers/Bears!"

Jake rolled his eyes. "So you think my getting laid is the answer?"

"Well, it's a start! You need to get your skinny white ass back out there!"

"Hey," Jake said smugly, "my skinny white ass has probably seen way more action than your sorry black one ever will."

"Now see, that's what I'm talking about! We need to get your swagger back, and I know just how to do it."

"Really?" Jake responded with an amused smile. "How?"

"We need to go on a pub crawl."

"A pub crawl?" Jake pushed himself up on his elbows. "Seriously?"

"Yeah. Why the hell not?"

Jake thought it over.

"Oh, God, no," Adrian groaned. "Not a pub crawl."

"Oh, what the hell," Jake conceded. "Why not?"

"Oh, I can think of about a million reasons why not, and that's just off the top of my head!" Adrian answered her husband's rhetorical question.

Pub crawling had been a regular thing for Jake and Charlie until Adrian came along. She had heard some stories about their notorious nights together, and she could only imagine what the uncut versions were.

But all that was behind them now, at least for Jake anyway, or so Adrian had thought. The mischievous gleam in her husband's eye and the smile he couldn't contain might now be proving her wrong.

"When?" Jake asked Charlie.

"Next Saturday night?"

"You're on."

"My man," Charlie fist-bumped his friend. "Let the games begin."

"Oh, shit," Adrian said while she threw her head back in defeat.

*

Jake's phone would not stop buzzing the entire way home. Charlie kept texting him about their game plan for next Saturday night.

Dude, Jake finally texted him back, *you're acting like a girl!*

Can't help it, man, Charlie wrote back. *The master is back!*

Jake laughed as he climbed up the stairs to his apartment. *Just because I said I'd do a pub crawl doesn't mean the master's back,* he thought. *Far from it.*

And I highly doubt this will be anything like our old pub crawls. Those turned into competitions between Charlie and me to see who could get the hottest girl in the bar to go home with him. And if there weren't any hotties in that bar, then we'd go to another one and so on and so on. The loser would be the one who ended up with a last call leftover. Jake grinned. *That never happened to me, though.*

"Do we really need to be hearing all this?" Adrian asked Kevin.

"We wouldn't still be here if we didn't," he answered.

It was easy, Jake continued while he unlocked the front door, *to give Charlie every gory detail the next day because I didn't care. The girls were just prizes. No, more like trophies. And I meant the same to them. There were no feelings involved. No worries about anyone's heart getting broken.*

It was all just a game. A game that I had gotten way too good at playing.

Jake had reached his bedroom. His phone still buzzed like it was about to explode. He couldn't take anymore, and neither could Adrian.

"Can't you put that thing someplace where we can't hear it anymore?" she said to her husband.

Jake opened the drawer of the nightstand and was about to toss the phone in it when he saw their wedding picture there, face down just the way he had left it.

His hands faltered when he grabbed it and flipped it over.

Then I met Adrian. Game over.

Jake seemed hypnotized by that photograph. His fingertips glided over the glass. A small part of him foolishly believed that if he did it just right, maybe he could bring her back to life.

Don't be such a pussy!

Adrian couldn't believe her ears. The thought was in her husband's mind, but it wasn't his voice.

The memory came out of nowhere. Jake must've been about thirteen years old. He had told his dad, during one of their many phone conversations, how nervous he was about talking to this girl he really liked.

"Don't be such a pussy!" Kevin had told him.

Kevin felt the heat from Adrian's glare.

"I know, bad choice of words," he said without looking at her, "but it's the truth."

Adrian rolled her eyes while the memory played out in Jake's mind.

"You're a Riley man, remember," Kevin told him.

"Yes, sir," Jake replied halfheartedly.

"Oh, c'mon; you can do better than that. Now say it like you mean it."

"Yes, sir!"

"That's my boy! And remember, Riley men never let anything get to them, especially girls, right?"

"Yes, sir!"

Maybe you were right, Dad, Jake thought now.

"What? No, he's not!" Adrian protested. "I'm your wife, not some pre-teen crush! You need to grieve for me."

"Adrian," Kevin warned her.

"What?" she snapped. "Am I wrong? Isn't that why we're here? To let him know it's okay to let it all out? That it won't make him 'a pussy' in your words?"

"Yes, but you're letting your emotions get the best of you again, and that's not going to help him either."

Adrian bit her tongue and took a deep breath.

"I'm sorry, sweet thing," Jake said as he put their picture back in the drawer, "but I can't hold on to you like this forever."

"Now what is that supposed to mean?" Adrian exclaimed.

Chapter Eighteen

"We're going to have a good time tonight."

Jake was talking to Charlie and trying to convince himself at the same time.

"No doubt, man," Charlie agreed as they bumped fists. "As always."

Charlie had picked Jake up. They were headed downtown to Broadway, an area well-known for trying to reinvent itself every few months with a new insurgence of bars and nightclubs. Jake hadn't been to this side of town since he had met Adrian. He felt like a tourist in a foreign country now.

"What happened to The Afterburner?" he asked Charlie.

"Burnt down about two years ago," Charlie answered while he pulled into a parking lot.

"The Red Zone?"

"Owners sold it and moved down south last winter. I think it's some kind of yuppie coffee bar or something now."

"The Outback?"

"Where have you been, man? They got shut down by the cops for serving minors months ago."

"Damn."

"Dude, relax. There's still plenty of places for us to hit."

An uneasy feeling settled in the pit of Jake's stomach as he stepped out of Charlie's truck. Kevin gave Adrian the evil eye.

"Why are you looking at me like that?" she asked him. "I'm just tagging along here, same as you."

The guys crossed the snow-covered street. They kept their heads down while they walked against the biting wind. Jake looked up when Charlie stopped in the doorway of one of the clubs. The hip-hop music was so loud inside that it threatened to blow the glass out of the windowpanes.

"Really?" Jake asked.

"What? Dude, this place is probably crawling with hot chicks."

"Yeah, but we won't be able to talk to any of them over all that noise."

"There are other ways to communicate with the ladies, you know."

"Oh, I know," Jake teased him. "I just never thought you did."

"Hey, I've upped my game since you've been on the sidelines."

"We'll see about that."

"So," Charlie paused to blow warm air into his cupped hands, "where would you like to start this evening's festivities?"

Jake glanced over his shoulder at the vast number of bars that surrounded them.

"How about The Left End? It's still here, isn't it?"

"Yeah," Charlie laughed, "it is."

Jake heard a tinge of disappointment in his friend's voice. "What's wrong?"

"Nothing. The Left End is just a little tamer than what I had in mind for you, but it's okay. This is your first night back. I'm up for whatever you want to do."

"Good, because I want to get inside and get a drink before I freeze my balls off!"

Charlie ordered two shots of whiskey for them as soon as they got up to the bar. Charlie held his high in the air while Jake's remained on the bar.

"C'mon, man; don't leave me hanging. Unless, of course, you're not man enough anymore."

"Oh no," Adrian said.

That's all it took. Jake downed that shot like the pro he used to be. Charlie watched him with proud papa eyes.

"Now what?" he asked Jake.

"Pool?"

"Let's do it. You rack 'em up, and I'll get us some beers."

"Pool is good, right?" Adrian asked Kevin as they followed Jake. "I mean, what kind of trouble could he possibly get into shooting pool?"

Jake was so intent on setting up the table that he never saw the pretty brunette saunter over to him, but Adrian did.

"What the hell does she think she's doing?"

"I believe they call it flirting," Kevin answered sarcastically.

"Are you looking for someone to play with?" the woman asked Jake while she set her drink on the edge of the table.

Curiosity caused Jake to raise his eyes up slowly to meet hers. Her cheeks instantly reddened.

"Pool," she blurted out. "I meant to play pool with."

Jake grinned. "Well, my buddy and I, we're just about to shoot a game, but you're more than welcome to play the winner."

"Oh, my God," Adrian said. "He's actually flirting back!"

"Easy there, Tiger," Kevin told her.

"I'm fine. I'm fine."

"Or we could play teams. You and me against your friend and mine maybe?" the woman suggested.

"She's got a friend too?" Adrian sounded appalled.

Charlie was just as shocked as Adrian when he came over with their beers.

Damn. They're drawn to him like bees to honey.

Adrian sat slumped over in her chair beneath a mounted twelve-point buck strung haphazardly with Christmas lights. The round of beers turned into a pitcher; the game of pool a tournament. Then Jake's partner made a move that got Adrian's attention.

Sylvie…Susie…Selfie. Adrian couldn't remember the girl's name, nor did she care. The girl stood alongside Jake and waited for Charlie and his partner to make their next shot. One hand was on her pool stick while the other one slid not so discreetly into the back pocket of Jake's jeans.

Adrian rocketed out of her chair after she saw her husband's reaction. He didn't seem to mind where Selfie's hand was at all. Kevin had to hold Adrian back. The lights on the deer blinked bright green.

"I know this is hell for you to watch," Kevin said, "but you've got to let it play out. For his own good."

Adrian's face fell. Kevin waited to release her until he was sure she had settled down. The lights returned to their steady glow. Charlie and Jake exchanged wolfish grins from across the pool table. Adrian sat back in her chair and felt like she was about to throw up.

*

Cassie burst through the doors of the ambulance garage with Max not far behind her.

"Cassie, wait; please," he pleaded. "Give me a chance to explain!"

"That's all right," Cassie shouted back at him while she stomped through the freshly fallen snow. "You made yourself perfectly clear in that letter you wrote to the board. I am obviously not ready to come back to work yet!"

"No, Cass," Max replied dejectedly, "you're not."

She stopped dead in her tracks. "How can you say that?" she asked as she spun around to face him. "I've done everything I was supposed to do!"

"That doesn't matter. You can jump through all the hoops you want, but I still can't clear you to come back until I know you're mentally ready to handle it."

"And what makes you such an expert on me all of a sudden, huh?"

"I'm your partner, remember. We've worked together long enough for me to know when something's off with you even if you won't admit it to yourself."

"You don't know shit about me!"

Max tipped his head back in frustration as Cassie stormed off.

Cassie jammed her hand into the pocket of her beige wool coat to retrieve her car keys. Adrian's mind instantly flashed back to the night of her death.

"We can't let her drive," Adrian told Kevin. "Not when she's this angry."

Kevin gave her a sympathetic smile. "Relax."

"Relax? How can I relax…?"

"Have faith."

Cassie got into the driver's seat and stuck the keys in the ignition. Her hands rested atop the steering wheel while she watched the snowflakes fall harder and heavier to the ground.

Is it really worth it to attempt to drive through this?

"No," Adrian yelled at her.

Hell, yeah! Maybe I'll even do a couple of donuts in the parking lot before I leave.

Cassie turned the key, but nothing happened.

"What?" Cassie asked. "You've got to be kidding me."

She tried again. Still nothing. Adrian breathed a sigh of relief.

"Thank you," she said to Kevin.

"What? I didn't do anything," he replied with a twinkle in his eye. "It's those damn car batteries. They sure don't make them like they used to."

Cassie grabbed her keys, jumped out of the car, and went to lock it when she stopped.

Screw it. If somebody wants it, they can have it. It's not like they're going to get very far with it anyway.

So now what?

She could grab a taxi or call someone to come get her, but she wasn't in the mood to head home. She needed to walk off her anger, and if a bar happened to pop up along her path, so be it. A drink, or three, didn't sound so bad right now.

*

A gust of wind slapped Cassie in the face. It was all the incentive she needed to move briskly down the street. She headed straight for the first flashing neon light she saw.

Cassie felt like every eye in the place was on her as she stood in the doorway and shook the snow off her hair and coat.

She scanned the crowded bar for an opening. There was none to be had, until a short, chubby, older guy with graying hair and a goatee waved her over.

"C'mon, darling," he told Cassie. "Don't be shy. There's plenty of room right here for you."

Oh, if I didn't need a drink so bad, Cassie thought to herself.

She gritted her teeth and plastered a smile onto her face.

"Thank you," she said while she made sure not to get too close to him so he wouldn't get the wrong idea.

"What'll you have?" the bartender asked her.

"A shot of Jose Cuervo, and keep 'em coming," Cassie replied.

"Rough day?"

"You have no idea."

The bartender poured Cassie's shot in front of her. She pushed her money across the bar to him, but he waved her off. She raised her glass to him in thanks.

Cassie downed it in one quick gulp. She cringed as it made its painful descent down her throat, but she grinned once it warmed her and drowned a few memories.

Cassie set the glass back down, intent on having another, when she saw something in the mirror behind the bar.

She leaned in closer and squinted.

No way! It can't be!

There, on the other side of the bar, was Jake pressed up against some little brunette as they tried to make a pool shot together.

Cassie's blood boiled as she took another look in the mirror. No doubt about it; it was him.

"You ready for another one?" the bartender asked her.

"Yeah, but could you do me a favor?"

"Sure."

"Make it one of your cheapest tequilas this time."

The bartender gave Cassie a strange look, but he did what she asked him to.

"Thanks."

Cassie slipped away over to the pool tables with her shot in hand. Charlie was the first to notice her.

"Hey, Cass! Long time no see."

"Cass!" Jake gave her a lopsided grin. "What are you doing here?"

"You son-of-a-bitch," Cassie said as she threw the shot in Jake's face.

"Whoa," Sylvie stood with her hands up in front of her. "This is way too much drama for me. C'mon, Cami; let's get the hell out of here."

"I'm right behind you," her friend agreed.

Charlie nearly tripped over his pool stick as he chased after them.

"Ladies, please, wait! I can explain everything!"

Jake stood there and bit his lip while the tequila dripped down his face.

"Now," Adrian said to Kevin, "if a guy would've done that to Jake…."

"My boy would've mopped the floor with him."

"Exactly."

Cassie bolted for the front door; Jake chased after her.

He called out to her several times, but she just kept going until he screamed out her name.

"What?" Cassie screamed back as she spun around on the sidewalk to face him.

"I wasn't going to sleep with her. We were just doing a little shameless flirting, that's all. Yeah, I'll admit it felt good, but I swear…."

Jake's voice trailed off when he saw the hopelessness in her eyes.

"This isn't just about you," Adrian told him.

"Where's your car at?" Jake asked.

Cassie's shoulders sagged. "Dead," her voice fell flat, "in St. Anne's parking lot."

Well, Jake thought, *that explains a lot.*

"Hmm," was all Jake said before he stepped out into the street and flagged down a cab.

"Get in," he told her as he held open the back door.

"With you? I don't think so."

"I wasn't asking."

Another cold blast of wind blew through Cassie.

"Now is really not a good time to be digging in your heels," Adrian advised her.

"Fine," Cassie huffed as she stomped into the cab.

"Where to?" the cabbie asked.

"Ashland and 119th," Jake told him.

"Your place?"

Cassie shot Jake a look that did nothing to intimidate him.

"It's closer," he answered matter-of-factly. *And there's something going on with you, and there's no way in hell I'm leaving you alone.*

The cabbie braked for a red light. They sat silently in their separate corners and stared out their windows.

The snow was coming down heavier now, but that still didn't stop the hot dog vendors from setting up their carts on the corners. A group of coeds strolled through the intersection on their way to one. They laughed and threw snowballs at each other, oblivious to the storm that brewed around them.

Must be nice, Jake thought, *not to have a care in the world.*

The light turned green and the cab was off and running again.

The traffic and the downtown lights quickly faded into the darkness as they approached the on ramp to the near-empty freeway.

Adrian looked anxiously behind her at Cassie and Jake. They didn't need to see it to know exactly where they were. They just knew.

Cassie hugged herself while she sank lower in her seat. Jake avoided the window altogether.

He saw a single tear trickle down Cassie's cheek and heard the sniffles she couldn't hold back. He reached across the seat for her hand. She unclenched her fist to take it, and that's how they remained for the rest of the ride back to Jake's apartment.

Adrian sat uneasily in the taxi and watched as Jake led a reluctant Cassie around the newly-formed snowdrifts and up the stairs.

"You okay?" Kevin asked as he ducked his head inside the window of the cab.

"Yeah," Adrian replied.

"Because you look a little green."

"I said I'm fine," Adrian snapped.

"All right, let's get going."

They appeared in the kitchen seconds later. Cassie dropped into the nearest chair while Jake hunched over the open refrigerator. He looked over his shoulder and froze when he saw Cassie with her head in her hands.

Oh, shit, Jake thought. *Please don't let her be doing what I think she's doing.*

"There's nothing Jake hates more…" Adrian began.

"…than to see a woman cry," Kevin finished.

Jake approached Cassie hesitantly. "You okay?" he asked as he set a bottle of beer down in front of her.

"No," she mumbled. "What if Max is right? What if they all are? What if I'm not ready? What if I never will be?"

"Whoa, whoa, whoa. Slow down," he said as he took a seat. "You got to catch me up to speed here."

Cassie sighed. "There was a meeting tonight about my reinstatement."

"Oh." Jake leaned back in his chair. "And I'm guessing it didn't work out the way you had hoped?"

"They extended my leave of absence. They said they'd review my case again in another six weeks." Cassie scoffed. "Six more weeks. How's more time off supposed to help me? I'm going stir crazy as it is. But that's not even the worst part.... It was a unanimous decision. Even my partner, Max, agreed." Her eyes fixated on the label of her beer. "I was so pissed off at him. I couldn't understand why he would do something like that to me until...." Cassie's voice trailed off.

"Until?" Jake prodded her.

She swallowed hard. "The ride back here."

A heavy silence hung over the room. Jake didn't know what to say, but he couldn't take much more of the quiet either.

"Don't be afraid to talk to her," Adrian told him.

I am not afraid!

"It'll get better," were the only words of encouragement Jake could come up with for Cassie.

I'm just not the greatest pep talker in the world.

"What if it doesn't?" Cassie asked.

"It will."

"You don't know that. I can't even get on that freeway without being haunted by that night. What's going to happen if I get called out there for another emergency? What am I going to do?"

"You'll handle it."

"I don't know how much more I can handle. This isn't just a job for me. I've fought too hard for this. To have it taken away from me now...." Her lips trembled. "I can't lose it. I just can't. I won't have anything left."

Cassie's hand splayed out across her face like a spiderweb.

"Stop," Jake said as he gently pulled her hand aside.

Her eyes stayed shut until he lifted her chin up with his fingertip and forced her to look at him.

"You'll always have me," he said sincerely.

They held each other's gaze for what felt like an eternity to Adrian.

"That look," Adrian's voice caught in her throat. "That's the same way he used to look at me."

She leaned into Kevin while her husband and best friend inched closer to each other. When their lips finally met, it wasn't in some passion-crazed, alcohol-induced kiss. It was soft and sweet and real. And far more painful for Adrian. She buried her face in Kevin's chest.

"C'mon," Kevin said as he held her tight. "Let's get you out of here."

The next thing Adrian knew, they were standing in the middle of Laura's living room. The only light came from the glow of the flat screen TV on the wall.

"What are we doing here?" Adrian asked Kevin.

"Practicing what I've been preaching," Kevin answered.

Laura entered the room with a huge bowl of popcorn and a glass of wine in her hands. She set everything down on the coffee table beside her before she pulled the fleece blanket off the back of the couch and wrapped herself up inside it to watch her movie.

Adrian turned to Kevin in confusion. "I don't get it."

"You will," Kevin replied while he made himself comfortable on the couch beside his wife. "Go on; have a seat. You'll love this one."

"Why not? At least it'll take my mind off what's going on in my apartment right now."

Adrian shuttered at the thought. She expected to get reamed by Kevin for what she had just said, but he didn't say a word. His mind seemed to be elsewhere.

"So what are we watching?" Adrian asked as she sat down cross-legged on the floor.

"*Mystic Pizza*," Kevin answered.

The tone of his voice made Adrian think there was more to it. She tried to read his mind, but he wasn't giving anything away.

"That's Laura's favorite movie, right?"

"It is," Kevin answered curtly.

"Okay," Adrian mumbled. "Pass the popcorn."

The sound of footsteps on the stairs caught Adrian's attention. She whirled around to see Clint standing in the entranceway.

"There you are," he said to his wife.

Laura sat up and paused the movie.

"Hey," she said as she looked sheepishly back at him.

"What are you doing down here so late?"

She shrugged. "I couldn't sleep. So I thought I'd come downstairs and watch a movie. I didn't want to wake you up."

"I rolled over and you weren't there. I just wanted to make sure you were okay."

Adrian was surprised to hear Kevin snicker at that.

"Well, well, well," she teased him. "It's not easy being green, is it?"

Adrian's smile vanished once Kevin glared at her.

"Sorry. Won't happen again."

"Mm-hmm."

"So what'cha watching?" Clint asked Laura. "Anything good?"

"Oh, nothing you'd be in to," Laura answered nervously.

Clint caught a glimpse of the movie case just as Laura tried to tuck it discreetly underneath her blanket. His face fell.

"Well, I'll let you get back to it." He gave her a peck on the cheek. "Don't stay up too late now."

"I won't."

Laura's face was riddled with guilt before her husband even turned away from her.

"All right," Adrian said to Kevin, "what is it with this movie?"

Kevin sighed. "I took her to see it on our first date, and even though I was never really a big fan of it, it sort of became our movie, so...."

"So, Clint's never allowed to watch it with her because of that?"

"Of course he's allowed. It's just up to Laura whether or not she wants him to."

"Uh-huh."

Kevin gave Adrian a dirty look. "It's like an unspoken rule between the two of them. I had nothing to do with it."

"Then why do I feel like you've influenced her decision on this somehow?"

"How many times do I have to tell you? Everybody's got free will, but," he stared affectionately at his wife, "maybe this is one thing I wanted to keep just between us."

"I knew it!"

"Until now."

"Wait. What?"

Adrian watched as Kevin reached for Laura. He stroked the side of her face with the back of his fingertips from the tip of her earlobe to her chin. Laura twitched as she felt a strange sensation run along her jaw line.

Kevin's fingers continued to glide down the length of her neck until they curled around her gold chain and captured her wedding ring.

Laura's hand was instantly drawn to it. Kevin froze when he felt his wife's touch.

"It's all right," he told her as he reluctantly pulled his hand out from underneath hers.

It's all right, she thought to herself while she stared pensively down at her ring.

"Hey, hon," Laura called out to Clint.

He stood at the foot of the stairs. "Yeah?"

"I made some room here for you if you want to come join me."

Clint peeked around the corner. "Really?"

"Mm-hmm," Laura smiled as she patted the seat beside her.

Clint tried to act casual as he bounded into the living room while Kevin gave up his spot on the couch.

"So," Clint said as he grabbed a handful of popcorn and sat down, "what's this movie about again?"

Laura's face practically glowed as she stared up at him. "I love you," she told him.

"I love you too," he replied as he kissed her softly on the lips.

"So," Laura began as she snuggled into Clint, "the movie's about two sisters, Kat and Daisy, and their best friend, Jojo. They all live in Mystic, Connecticut...."

That was as much as Adrian heard before she and Kevin disappeared.

Chapter Nineteen

Sunlight poured through the windows, but it was anything but a good morning for Adrian. She sat in her rocking chair with her knees pulled up to her chin and watched them as they slept together on the hide-a-bed.

"You all right?" Kevin asked her.

"I was just about to ask you that," she replied.

"I'll be fine," Kevin said as he stood up and stretched. "That's the toughest part about this job you know."

"I know," Adrian grumbled while her head fell onto her knees.

"But the longer we hold on to them, the harder it is to let go. Believe me."

She looked up and watched Kevin stare blankly out the patio doors.

"Could've been worse. At least Clint wasn't your best friend."

Kevin turned to her. "You think it would've been any easier for you if he would've brought that girl from the bar home with him instead?"

"Yes. No. I don't know!" Adrian brought her hands to her forehead. "I want Jake to be happy. I really do, but...."

"Hey, you don't need to explain anything to me."

There was movement from the bed. Cassie rolled toward them. The sunlight warmed her face while a smile formed on her lips.

Her mind was lost in that sweet, simple, intoxicating kiss.

"Oh, my God." Adrian clutched her stomach. "I think I'm going to be sick."

Cassie burrowed deeper beneath the covers in a desperate attempt to remain in the moment.

"Wait a minute," Adrian said. "She doesn't think that was all just a dream, does she?"

Cassie's eyes popped open when she suddenly felt a strong arm wrap around her.

"Not anymore," Kevin answered.

Bits and pieces of the night before slowly came together in Cassie's mind. *The meeting...the fight with Max...the stupid car dying...walking to that bar...that girl with Jake...Jake....*

JAKE!

Cassie sat up abruptly and stared down, horrified by the man who lay beside her.

She felt like she couldn't breathe, especially after she pulled the sheets up tighter to her naked body.

Cassie needed to get out of there...now. But how? Her car was stuck downtown, if it was even still there.

First things first. Let's just get the hell out of here before he wakes up.

She squirmed out of his embrace and crept toward the edge of the bed. Cassie glanced back; Jake barely moved.

She faced forward; her head hung low when she saw their clothes scattered across the floor.

Cassie slipped wearily into her underwear and jeans before she grabbed the rest of her things and made a beeline for the bathroom.

"This her first walk of shame?" Kevin asked Adrian.

"First one I know of," Adrian answered.

Cassie locked the door and stared hard at her reflection in the mirror.

How? How could you do this? She shook her head. *No! There was no time for judgment calls right now.*

She fished through her purse for her cell phone and once she found it she scrolled frantically through her contacts. Her finger hovered over "Mom" and "Maggie."

Uh-uh. Nope, Cassie thought. *There's no way in hell I'm calling my mom to come get me. It would be one long, never-ending lecture. No thank you. Plus, once I tell Maggie about my car, she'll make Tony come with us to help get it running again. Now let's hope she picks up her phone.*

Thankfully, Maggie did and she agreed to come rescue Cassie. No questions asked.

Cassie leaned over the sink and scrubbed her makeup-smeared face clean.

If only I could do the same to my conscience.

All right. Enough!

"I had nothing to do with that last part," Adrian immediately told Kevin.

"I know you didn't," he replied quietly.

Cassie threw on her coat and left the bathroom. She paused at the end of the hallway and breathed a sigh of relief when she heard Jake snoring like a freight train.

Thank God he's not a light sleeper, Cassie thought to herself as she snuck out the front door.

Jake's snoring suddenly ceased after the car pulled away from the curb.

Thank God, he thought as he sat up and rubbed his hands over his face. *I didn't know how much longer I could keep that act up.*

"What?" Adrian's mouth fell open. "He was faking it?"

Jake's thoughts suddenly shifted to Adrian and her picture mornings. *She always wanted to catch me so badly, but I just couldn't help it. I always heard her moving around on the bed, no matter how quiet or sneaky she thought she was being. I can't believe she never caught on to that. But knowing her, she was probably too focused on the shot.*

Truth is, I loved listening to her work. The way she tip-toed around the room to find just the right angle...how she swore under her breath whenever something wasn't going right...the excitement in her voice right before she took the shot. He chuckled. *Like she was about to orgasm.*

Adrian blushed. "He heard all that?"

"He did," Kevin answered.

It almost made me wish she did get that perfect shot of me. Almost. I just couldn't resist scaring the shit out of her either. I figured she'd always have plenty of other chances to really catch me.

Jake's cell phone rang and saved him from any further deep thinking. He cringed when he saw the caller ID. It was Charlie.

What the hell am I gonna tell him now?

"Dude!" Charlie was so excited he sounded like he might come right through the phone.

Jake laughed despite himself. "What happened, man?"

"What happened?" Charlie asked incredulously. "I got the fuck of my life last night; that's what happened!"

Jake couldn't resist. "And then you woke up, right?"

"No, asshole," Charlie replied good-naturedly. "It really happened. I swear."

"I'll believe it when I hear it."

"Oh, you're going to hear all about it, man, as soon as I pick you up."

"Pick me up? For what?"

"Seriously? Have you not looked out your windows at all yet?"

"It hasn't been one of my top priorities, no."

"Snowstorm Cassandra's in full force; they're predicting at least another six to ten inches by tonight."

"Jesus," Jake groaned.

Charlie and Jake had been working for the City of Ashwaubenon for about two years now. Charlie knew a friend who knew a friend who had connections that got them both jobs. The timing couldn't have been better; Jake had been stressing out at that time about how in the world he was going to afford to marry Adrian. The only downside was in the winter when major snowstorms like this hit.

"So it's off to plow we go," Charlie said all too cheerfully. "I'll see you in twenty, dude."

"Yeah, all right," Jake mumbled.

Charlie launched into his torrid tale as soon as Jake got into his truck. He held nothing back either. Adrian knew details meant something completely different to men than they did to women, but she never realized just how much until she heard Charlie's story.

Her jaw dropped in disgust.

"Really?" she groaned to Kevin.

"This is Charlie talking, remember."

"I know, but still."

"So," Charlie said, after he finished his story, "now it's your turn."

"My turn?" Jake asked. "For what?"

"To tell me all about your night."

Shit! How am I gonna play this?

I could tell him the truth, right down to the last gory detail like in the old days.

Jake tried but the words stalled on his tongue.

"You did get laid last night, didn't you?"

"Well, yeah," Jake responded as if the answer were obvious. *That much I can admit to.*

"And?"

"And what?"

"Details, man! Give me details!"

Jake found himself speechless once more.

"You're being awfully quiet, dude, which can only mean one of two things: the chic was really awful in the sack or…."

"Or what?"

"Or…." Charlie left a dramatic pause, "you're holding out on me."

Jake let out a sigh of relief without even realizing he had held his breath.

"Maybe I just didn't want to steal your thunder," Jake told him.

"Bullshit!" Charlie laughed. "You just want to torture me; that's all. Whatever, man. Two can play this game. It don't bother me at all. I can wait. I know I'll get it out of you sooner or later."

"Yeah, okay; whatever, man."

Charlie just laughed. He kept one eye on the road in front of him and the other on his best friend.

Damn, Charlie thought. *My boy's been struck again.*

"What is he talking about?" Adrian stammered.

That's the only other explanation I got, Charlie continued. *I mean, why else wouldn't he kiss and tell? The only other time he ever clammed up like that on me was after he'd been with Adrian.*

"What?" Adrian couldn't believe her ears.

She looked to Kevin for an explanation, but he didn't have one for her. Then she turned to her husband, who still seemed to be going through some inner turmoil of his own.

He let it go. Charlie never lets anything like that go. He's like a pit bull for Christ's sake, especially when it comes to this.

Aw, shit! What if he knows?

Adrian's face went pale.

But how could he? He was too busy chasing after those girls to see me get into the cab with Cassie.

Some of the color returned to Adrian's face.

So why didn't I just tell him what happened and change the names to protect the innocent?

"Yeah, why not?" Adrian asked the question out loud before she could stop herself.

Because it was Cassie, Jake thought. *That's why.*

Adrian's heart sank.

"And just what exactly does that mean?" she asked.

It would've been so much easier, Jake continued, *if I had just brought that girl from the bar home with me instead. I could've told Charlie everything. The words would've rolled right off my tongue no problem because she didn't mean anything to me. She would've just been another conquest for me to brag about—another chapter to add to the legend of "The Master."*

And then Cassie showed up.

They had just reached the city garage. Jake leapt out of Charlie's truck as if his seat were on fire. *None of this would've ever happened if I wouldn't have gone out drinking with Charlie.*

"Yeah, okay; you just keep telling yourself that."

Adrian's eyes nearly popped out of her head.

"Kevin, how could you say that?"

"What?" Kevin responded calmly. "It's the truth."

Jake stood out in the storm, his head tilted back while the snowflakes pelted his face. His father's imposing voice suddenly loomed large in his mind:

Be a man and take responsibility for your own actions.

Jake remembered getting that speech from his dad after he got caught smoking in the boys' bathroom with a bunch of his buddies back in junior high.

That's how I knew I really screwed up—when mom wouldn't do anything to punish me and made me wait to talk to dad about it instead.

I kept telling him it wasn't my fault. That my friends pressured me into doing it, but he wasn't buying any of it.

"Whoa, whoa, whoa! Hold it right there!" Kevin had told his son. "You're not a little boy anymore, Jacob. You can't blame anyone else for something you did. You need to own up to it. Be a man and take responsibility for your own actions."

"Dude," Charlie suddenly yelled to Jake, "c'mon; we got to get going!"

And that's exactly what I need to do now, Jake thought as he wiped the snow off his face. Be *responsible for my own actions.*

*

Maggie and Tony came running as soon as Maggie got Cassie's text. They picked her up from Jake's and drove downtown to find her car safe and sound in the parking lot right where she had left it the night before.

"Why," Cassie moaned as she tipped her head backward, "did I go into that damn bar? Why didn't I just call a cab to take me to The Borderline or, better yet, just go home?"

"Enough," Maggie gently scolded her.

They sat across from each other in a booth at a twenty-four-hour diner. Maggie offered to buy Cassie breakfast while they waited for Tony to fix her car.

This was about the third chorus of Cassie's whoa-is-me song that Maggie had heard from her since they had picked her up.

"What's done is done, and if you ask me," Maggie added over the rim of her coffee cup, "maybe it was meant to happen."

Cassie lowered her eyes at her in disbelief. "So, what, you think I was meant to have a one-night-stand with my best friend's husband?"

"Oh, please." Maggie shot the same look right back at her. "I've known you long enough to know you're not that kind of girl. Hell, I've seen you flat-out shit-faced before, and even then, it still didn't cross your mind to go jump some guy's bones."

Maggie gave their waitress a goofy grin as she set the food down in front of them. Cassie touched her fingers to her temple and shook her head.

"It's just not you," Maggie concluded after their waitress left.

"So what are you saying?"

Maggie gave her a comforting smile. "I'm saying that there's something there, darling. I've seen it every time the two of you have been together lately."

Cassie tried to blow it off, but her eyes gave her away.

"And I'm guessing you've felt it too, huh?"

Adrian leaned in close, eager to hear her friend's response. Cassie didn't know what to say.

"But I...I can't feel like that. Not about Jake!"

"Why not?"

"Why not? Because he's Jake; our Jake; Adrian's Jake! She'd come back from the dead just to kill me if she knew about this!"

Adrian's cheeks flushed bright red.

"Did you go gunning for him? Did you have some sort of evil plan to start seducing him in the hospital or something?"

"No! There was no plan! It just..."

"...happened, right?"

Cassie chewed her lip while she mulled this over. "Mm-hmm."

"Well, I think wherever Adrian is right now," Maggie said as she took Cassie's hand, "she knows that too. And I'm sure she's okay with it."

Adrian had a hard time swallowing the lump that suddenly constricted her throat.

Tony slid in beside Maggie in the booth. "Car's ready to roll whenever you ladies are."

Tony insisted on following Cassie back to her apartment just in case she had any other car issues. Maggie walked Cassie to her front door while Tony waited in the truck.

"You good? Because I can stay if you need me to. Tony won't mind coming back for me."

"Naw, I'll be fine," Cassie replied.

"All right," Maggie replied reluctantly. "Just promise me you'll call or stop in the bar if you change your mind, okay?"

"Yes, Mom," Cassie teased before she gave Maggie a hug. "And thanks again for everything."

"Anytime, kiddo. Anytime," Maggie told her before she left.

Cassie stepped inside and leaned back against the doorframe.

She still wasn't convinced Adrian would've given her blessing about any of this.

"What are you doing?" Adrian asked Kevin as a thought popped into Cassie's head.

"Just making a suggestion," he replied.

What? No! Cassie thought. *That's crazy! But then again...what have I got to lose, right?*

Chapter Twenty

The closer Cassie got, the slower the wheels on her Grand Am turned. She hadn't been here since the funeral. She just couldn't, and it felt even worse now.

Maybe this wasn't such a hot idea after all.

Cassie shifted the car into park and rested her chin on the steering wheel as she stared out into the cemetery.

"You can do this," Kevin told her.

"I can do this," Cassie told herself.

She took a deep breath and jumped out of the car before her nerves got the better of her again.

She wrapped her coat tighter around her waist, even though it was nowhere near as cold as it had been the day before. Her boots sunk deep into the snow as she trudged down the aisle.

Of course they wouldn't have this plowed. I'm probably the only idiot who comes out here this time of year.

Cassie came to an abrupt halt. Her ranting ceased; her heart suddenly felt as if it were gripped in a vise.

She knelt down to wipe the mounds of snow off the tombstone with her gloved hand. It was one thing to talk about Adrian's death, but it became so much more real to her when she saw it etched in stone:

Adrian Elizabeth Riley

April 10, 1989—July 21, 2015

Cassie crouched down and stared thoughtfully at her best friend's grave, unaware that Adrian stood right behind it and was watching her.

"Where do I start?" Cassie asked herself.

"I don't know." Adrian replied as she came around to the front of her headstone. "Just talk to me like we always do."

They sat across from each other in the snow like two teenagers about to dish out the best gossip they knew.

"I slept with him, Aide." Cassie lurched forward as if she were about to throw up. "I slept with Jake last night. I wish I could tell you it was all just a big mistake; blame it on the alcohol or the monumentally fucked up night I had, but I can't. I knew what I was doing. I wanted it to happen, and that's what makes this so much worse."

Cassie's eyes followed the path she had been tracing in the snow, but now she forced herself to look at the headstone as if she were face-to-face with her best friend.

"I have feelings for him, Aide, and it's scaring the shit out of me. They weren't always there, I swear."

"I know," Adrian said as she reached for her best friend's hand.

"It's just that I don't know what to do, and I thought maybe if I came here and talked to you, told you everything, you could help me figure it out somehow."

"Me too."

Cassie nearly jumped out of her skin when she heard Jake's voice. He stood behind her in his Carhartt jacket and work boots, a small bouquet of roses in his hands.

Adrian gave him a knowing smile.

"Ah, the apology bouquet," she said.

"I'm sorry," Jake said as he knelt down beside Cassie. The look in his eyes suggested he wasn't just talking about scaring her.

An awkward silence fell upon them. Cassie couldn't think; Jake found it difficult to speak.

"C'mon," Kevin urged his son. "Just tell her already."

The words suddenly spilled out of him.

"Cass, I love Adrian and I always will...."

Cassie felt as if her insides had suddenly been hollowed out.

Oh no! He's trying to let me down easy. I can't let him do this.

"I have to go," Cassie stammered.

She scrambled to her feet and rushed to her car before Jake even had a chance to stop her. He stood there dumbstruck and watched her go.

"What the hell are you doing?" Adrian asked him. "Don't just stand there! Go after her!"

"What's wrong?" Kevin asked Adrian as he walked around to the front of her grave. "Isn't this what you wanted?"

"Not if it means they're both miserable."

"Then do something to fix it."

*

Cassie's heart still pounded in her ears as she ran into her apartment, flung her open purse on the floor, and dived onto her bed. Adrian sat alongside her.

"Really?" Adrian asked, her voice filled with disappointment.

"I am such an idiot!" Cassie moaned into her pillow.

"Well, yeah," Adrian agreed, "if this is how you're going to handle it, you are."

Miranda Lambert's "Only Prettier"—Cassie's ringtone—started to play. Adrian followed the sound of the song until she found the phone underneath Cassie's bed. She pushed it out just enough so she could see the caller ID. It was Jake.

"So I suppose you're not going to answer that either, huh?" Adrian sat back on the bed and shook her head while Cassie pulled the blanket up further over her head. "No man is worth doing this to yourself over. Not even my husband."

That's when it came to Adrian. "Wait. That's it. You can't do this to yourself. We made a pact, remember?"

The pact.

Cassie groaned as her mind went back to that weekend.

It was their junior year of high school; one week before prom. Cassie was supposed to go with Danny Douglas—the captain of the football team—until he dumped her that Friday afternoon.

"Danny the Douchebag was more like it," Adrian said. "We found out later that he hooked up with some sorority girl who was home on spring break that weekend instead. Cass was a wreck. She locked herself in her room and wouldn't see or talk to anyone, even me. But I managed to wear her down."

Cassie giggled. *Adrian asked me, "What would Miranda do?"*

"Hey, it was a longshot, but it worked. You let me in, and I convinced you to come back to my house and have a bonfire where we burned everything that reminded you of that douchebag."

And that's when Adrian came up with the pact.

Adrian grinned. "We swore, over a shot of my dad's best whiskey, to look out for each other and to make sure that we never gave another man the power to destroy us like that again."

"All right, all right," Cassie poked her head out and stared up at the ceiling. "I get it. I'm on it."

She pushed the blanket off her and went to pick her phone up off the floor to call Jake. That was when she saw the box underneath her bed.

Cassie sat back on her knees and swallowed hard. "Only Prettier" erupted throughout the room again, but Cassie didn't even flinch. She was too zoned in on that box.

"Whoa," Adrian said. "Looks like it's more than just men we give the power to destroy us."

She got down on the floor beside Cassie. "C'mon. You've got this."

Cassie pulled the box out into the light along with a ton of cobwebs and dust bunnies.

Just rip off the Band-Aid, Cassie thought to herself.

She flipped the lid off and winced as if she expected a python to come slithering out.

"Wow!" Adrian said in amazement. "Would you look at that?"

Cassie opened first one eye, then the other as she turned reluctantly toward the box.

It was a hodgepodge of things most people would've considered junk, but it all held great sentimental value to Cassie, and it wasn't long before Adrian got caught up wandering down memory lane with her.

There was an assortment of old, faded bar napkins with illegible signatures on them. The girls shared a knowing grin.

Autographs!

"We got these whenever my dad let us come to any gigs The Uprising played at with some of our other favorite bands, but we'd only ask for the hottest guys' ones."

"Well, of course," Kevin replied sarcastically.

"And if we were really lucky, they'd give us their phone numbers too," Adrian added as she raised her eyebrows playfully up and down. "My dad always tried to confiscate those from us, but we managed to save a few."

Cassie dug deeper and found signed set lists, guitar picks, and ticket stubs; they still knew the name and specific performance for every single autograph Cassie pulled delicately from the box.

Summerfest 2003, Cassie reminisced as she examined a napkin from The Brew Factory. *We snuck behind the pavilion in-between acts to meet up with Jax and Jeremy, the drummer and bass player from* Road Block.

"They were twins, weren't they?" Adrian asked.

Cassie's smile widened. *Twins and older men; seniors in high school who really knew how to French kiss.*

"Damn, we had some epic summers, didn't we?" Adrian said proudly.

They wouldn't have been near as good without my partner in crime, though, Cassie thought.

And so it went. Each buddy photo, birthday card, wristband, and pressed penny brought back a fond memory. Cassie's phone rang like crazy, but she treated it like background noise to her treasure hunt.

It wasn't as bad as Cassie had feared, until she came across the picture that was taken the day she completed her EMT certification.

There had been a small ceremony afterwards. Everyone posed for pictures with their families—everyone, that is, except Cassie. Her parents weren't there.

"That's when I stepped in," Adrian said.

"C'mon," Adrian told Cassie as she dragged her toward the photographer. "It's family picture time."

"What?" Cassie asked.

"Look; just because your parents didn't deem this a worthy enough event to attend doesn't mean you don't have family here for you."

Cassie's eyes glistened with tears. "Thank you."

"I'm proud of you," Adrian told her while they hugged. "It takes a brave woman to follow her heart, and if your parents can't handle that, then screw them."

"When we posed for that picture," Adrian explained to Kevin, "we said 'screw them' instead of 'cheese'."

Cassie got lost in that photograph and what Adrian had told her.

It takes a brave woman to follow her heart.

Adrian put her hands on Cassie's shoulders and leaned in close. "If Jake is what your heart truly wants, don't let me stand in your way."

Cassie's head drooped as her eyes moved indecisively back and forth from the picture to her cell phone. She eventually set the picture back in the box and dialed Jake's number. Adrian stepped back and nodded.

Jake's phone went to voicemail.

Great. Now what do I do?

"Go find him," Adrian said softly.

Cassie got up, grabbed her keys, and headed for the front door. She threw it open, startled to find Jake standing there, his fist hung in mid-air, poised to knock.

They talked over each other until Jake captured Cassie's face in the palms of his hands and kissed her with everything he had.

The kiss sent Cassie's mind reeling. She embraced Jake and let all of her insecurities go, his lips her sole focus.

Adrian bit her lip, a resigned expression on her face as she squeezed past them on her way out the door.

Chapter Twenty-One

The tension rolled right off Sam's shoulders the second she shut her office door behind her.

She wrestled her arms out of her suit jacket and untucked her white silk blouse from her black skirt while she made a beeline for the mini-bar across the room. She grabbed the bottle of Chardonnay and filled her glass to the brim before she collapsed onto the coral-colored wraparound sofa.

Sam put her hand to her forehead as she stared out the full-length window at the frozen-over bay.

Some days, she thought as she tipped the glass back to take a long drink, *I wonder what ever possessed me to agree to teach a photography class.*

A look of contentment eased onto her face after she pried her eyes away from the window and onto the framed photographs that adorned the bright blue walls. Her mind instantly traveled back to the moment when she captured each one of those pictures.

The sun setting from the window of the top floor of The Cofrin Library after I finished teaching for the day; the Fourth of July fireworks finale exploding over the Fox River from the party boat I was invited on; laying back on the hood of my car at Austin Straubel Airport—my idea for fun on a Friday night—as a plane soared right in front of a golden full moon.

That's why. Because I wanted to nurture that same kind of passion for photography in the next generation. Be someone's mentor; inspire them to greatness.

Sam scoffed as she got up to pour herself another glass of wine. *Yeah, right. Most of them only sign up for the class because they think it'll be an easy A; the simplest way to fulfill their fine arts requirement. I can't count the number of times I've caught kids sleeping in class, or seen the glazed-over looks in their eyes when I'm giving a lecture on lighting or shadow techniques. Jesus, I can't even remember the last passionate photography student I taught.*

A bittersweet smile formed on Sam's lips as it came to her. *Adrian. Now there was a girl with real passion. I mean, c'mon, she charged out into thunderstorms with her camera for Christ's sake!*

Adrian did a double take.

"H-how did she even know about that?" she asked stunned.

I expected to see such great things from her, but now.... Sam shook her head in disappointment.

Adrian nearly fell off the end of the couch.

"Did she just...?"

"Yep," Kevin responded calmly while he strolled around the room admiring all the photographs.

"So Samantha Lancaster really did just...."

"Praise you?" Kevin stopped to glance back at Adrian. "Yes," he grinned, "she really just did."

"Holy...."

That's why I wanted to do this show. To give the world a chance to see what I saw in her work. She deserved that.

Adrian shook her head as if she were trying to clear it. "Are you sure I'm not hallucinating?" she asked Kevin.

"Positive."

I thought it was a good idea, Sam continued while she stared uncertainly at her phone, *but now I'm not so sure.*

"What?" Adrian asked breathlessly.

"Don't jump to conclusions," Kevin warned her. "Listen to everything she has to say first."

Adrian swallowed back her fear and waited for Sam to explain.

The show's supposed to open in a few weeks, but I've still got nothing from Jake.

Kevin gave Adrian a knowing look; she sunk humbly down in her seat.

It's like he's gone MIA or something. No pictures, no phone calls, no nothing. I should call him. That's what I would do with any other artist I was waiting on material from.

I'd call them up and let them know we have deadlines to meet! That it's not just their reputation at stake here but mine too! Shut down every lame excuse they throw at me; warn them that if they can't come through for me, I'll make sure they'll never have another show again!

Motivation by panic. It's always worked well for me in the past, but this time's different.

Jake's not an artist. My bitchy, business-woman bullshit won't work on him. He won't care what I say or do; he's got nothing to lose; this is his only show.

Sam sighed. *Maybe I should just cut my losses and cancel the whole thing while there's still time.*

"What? No!" Adrian protested. "Don't do that! Jake needs to do this. Don't let him off the hook so easily. Just call and nudge him along a little bit before you go and pull the plug on this. Please."

Or maybe I should just quit overreacting and call and talk to him first, Sam thought.

"Yes. Exactly. Don't jump to conclusions," Adrian said.

Kevin arched a suspicious eyebrow at Adrian.

"What?" Adrian asked him. "I'm just doling out some of your good advice. Aren't you proud of me? I've been listening to you."

"Uh-huh."

Sam chewed on her lip as she reached for the phone.

"Hello?"

Jake and Cassie were at The Borderline splitting a Mexican pizza when Sam called.

"Jake? Hey, it's Sam. I just thought I'd check in with you to see how you were coming with the pictures for Adrian's show."

His slice of pizza suddenly didn't taste as good to him as it had a moment ago. Jake chewed on it as if it were rubber.

"Um," he stammered while Cassie watched him, her eyes narrowed in concern. "Good."

"Really?"

"Yeah, in fact I should have it all finished by this weekend."

"You're not just blowing smoke up my ass now, are you?"

"No way, Sam," said Jake, sounding more confident than he felt. "I would never do that to you."

"Good. Glad to hear it."

"I'll see you soon."

"What's wrong?" Cassie asked him after he got off the phone.

"Nothing," Jake answered while he tried to go back to eating his pizza as if the phone had never rung. "That was just Sam."

"I got that. So was she calling about Adrian's pictures?"

"Yep."

"Oh."

Cassie kept her eyes lowered while she drank her margarita. It didn't go unnoticed by Jake.

"What?" he asked her.

"Nothing," Cassie mumbled.

"C'mon," Adrian urged her friend. "Now's not the time to clam up."

"You know, if you need any help with that…."

Cassie didn't even get the rest of her question out.

"I'm fine."

Jake spoke so sharply that Cassie's eyes leapt up to his.

"Okay," she shot back at him.

Jake bowed his head. "I'm sorry. It's just that…."

"It's all right. I get it. You need to do this on your own, just like I did."

Jake's eyebrows wrinkled in confusion.

"You remember me telling you about the box under my bed?" Cassie asked. "The one I hadn't looked at since Adrian died."

"Yeah?" *Sure.*

"I was going through it right before you came to my apartment that afternoon."

"Really?"

"Mm-hmm."

Jake's face remained impassive while inwardly she had shocked him. *Well, hell. If Cassie can do it, then so can I.*

*

Jake sat on his bedroom floor later that afternoon. The closet doors were open; all Adrian's photo albums surrounded him. A six-pack of beer, as well as his wife, was by his side. He was ready to go to work.

Jake decided to begin with the oldest albums first. He split everything up into two piles: the ones for the show and the ones not for the show. Adrian voiced her opinion too, but whether or not Jake took it was another story.

"Hey!" she protested at one point when Jake set a photo she was particularly fond of in the "don't use" pile. "C'mon. I love that one!"

"But apparently Jake doesn't," Kevin teased her as he lay back on their bed.

"And it's his choice now, not mine."

"Exactly."

"Dammit," Adrian grumbled half-jokingly.

Jake had his first beer gone before he got halfway through the first album.

Shit! I may need to go pick up another case.

His drinking eventually tapered off as both he and Adrian became more engrossed in the photographs and the memories they brought back.

Time passed quickly. Jake reached the last and most recent album before he knew it. Adrian bit down hard on her lip.

"What's wrong?" Kevin asked her.

"Nothing," Adrian lied.

Jake opened it from the back. He flipped through page after blank page before he finally found something.

Our last baseball game together.

"We went down to Chicago every spring to see the Cubs' home opener," Adrian explained to Kevin. "Jake could've cared less about baseball, but he knew how crazy I was about it."

Jake spread the album out on his lap. There were tons of pictures of Wrigley Field—inside and out—practically every statue around the ballpark, and all of the players, in the dugout, on the field, pre-game, post-game….

Adrian shrugged sheepishly. "So maybe I get a little carried away with the camera when I'm down there."

"You think?" Kevin teased her.

The funny thing is, Jake smiled as he plucked out a photograph of the team warming up from the album, *she could tell you every player's name and position like they were members of her family.*

Me? I had to keep looking at my program every ten minutes because I couldn't keep them all straight.

Jake placed the photograph back in its spot and moved on to the next page, unprepared for what he was about to see.

First was the requisite shot of Adrian standing by the entrance gate to Wrigley Field in her Sammy Sosa jersey, proudly waving her foam finger in the air; beside it was a picture of a little boy sitting on top of his dad's shoulders, high-fiving Clark, the Cubs' mascot, outside the ballpark; below that one were two little girls in the sand by the bleachers covered in dirt from the tops of their perfectly braided hair all the way down to their pink polished toenails and loving every minute of it; and the last photo was one of a newborn baby sleeping peacefully in its mother's arms while they stood for The National Anthem.

Jake slammed the album shut and jerked his head away, but he couldn't stop thinking about it. Adrian remained on the floor, her eyes intent upon her husband.

"You know," she said softly, "right before the accident, I thought that maybe I might be—"

"I know," Kevin said, his voice subdued.

Adrian went to hug her husband just as he snapped out of his daze.

Good enough, Jake thought as he stood abruptly up.

He called Sam the next day, told her he was finished, and asked whether she'd be around for him to drop them off.

She said she would be and gave him her address.

Jake was just about to go when Adrian thought of something.

"Wait! My camera. You got to take my camera, babe."

Jake stopped, his eyes drawn to the nightstand.

Take it. Please.

*

Sam didn't know what to say when Jake showed up at her door with Adrian's camera.

"I...uh...figured there might be something on here you could use too," he explained as he handed it over to her.

"Thank you."

Sam couldn't help but notice the way Jake's eyes lingered on the camera. It reminded her of the day he had first come to see her.

There he was, this big strapping man standing in my doorway looking more like a bodybuilder than my intern's fiancé.

I could tell Jake was at a loss, even though he refused to admit it to me. I had to bite my tongue to keep from giggling when he pulled this stack of folded up papers out of his jacket pocket.

He had been saving up to buy Adrian a camera.

Adrian's eyes softened. "My birthday present."

He didn't want to get her just any camera. He wanted the best, but he also wanted it to be a surprise for her. Jake knew he couldn't suddenly express an interest in camera styles without raising Adrian's suspicions,

so he started searching the Internet, which only left him more confused.
That's when he knew he needed professional help.

So he came to me. And I agreed to help him find the perfect one for
her on one condition: he was going to owe me a favor somewhere down
the line. I thought I could use him as free manual labor, not for something
like this.

"Don't worry," Sam said as her mind snapped back into the present.
"I promise I'll take good care of it for you."

"I know you will," Jake replied as he turned his stunning blue eyes
on her.

Sam caught a glimpse of something in Jake's eyes that made her want
to give him a great big bear hug, but she resisted the temptation. Her lips
curved up into a sympathetic smile instead.

This is wrong; so, so wrong," she thought to herself as she leaned
against the doorjamb and watched Jake head back to his truck.

Sam couldn't get into her office fast enough, but something held her
back once she sat down in front of her laptop.

This is Adrian's camera.

Sam knew how sacred a thing that was to any photographer, herself
included. She suddenly felt as if she were about to snoop inside the pages
of Adrian's journal.

"It's okay," Adrian told her. "There's nothing on there I wouldn't
want you or anyone else to see."

Sam retrieved the memory card from Adrian's camera. She inserted
it carefully into her computer, and reminded herself to breathe again
while the photographs downloaded. Adrian hovered over Sam's shoulder;
her heart leapt into her throat as all of the pictures she had taken that
morning of Jake suddenly appeared right before her eyes.

Adrian had always been her own worst critic, and she was even more so now. She second-guessed every decision Sam made, to the point where Adrian didn't even think there was anything useable on the entire roll of film. But then they came to the last photograph.

Sam leaned slowly back in her chair.

"That's it," she said, her voice filled with disappointment as if she had just come to the end of a really good book.

Adrian felt the same way.

"That's the last picture I'll ever take."

Inspiration suddenly struck Sam.

"That's it!"

Adrian watched Sam in awe as she leapt forward; her fingers flew across the keyboard in a crazed frenzy to keep up with all the ideas that bombarded her mind.

Oh...my...God! Adrian thought.

Chapter Twenty-Two

L aura sat in her son's driveway, her hands wrapped around the top of her steering wheel so tightly that her knuckles had turned pure white. She sighed heavily as she looked up at Jake's apartment.

There's no way around this. I need to talk to him about it. I've been putting it off long enough—something Clint reminds me of on a daily basis.

Maybe it won't be so bad. Yeah, right, Laura scoffed. *Because Jake won't have any problem at all with me asking him to give me away to Clint at our wedding. Nope, not at all.*

Laura let go of the steering wheel and ran her hands up and down her face.

"Lord," she said out loud, her eyes raised expectantly up to the sky, "give me strength."

It's going to be fine, Laura told herself as she walked up to the front door and knocked. *Just don't make more of it than it needs to be.*

"It's open," Jake shouted.

Laura sucked in one last sharp breath of air before she turned the knob and ventured inside.

Jake sat in the kitchen flipping through his mail when she came in.

194 The Last Photograph

He tossed whatever was left in his hand onto the table; then he draped his arm over the top of the chair.

"Hey," he said, his chin on his elbow and his eyes zeroed in on the large container his mother held in her hands. "So, you got anything good in there for me?"

"Nah, not really. Just some homemade tiramisu that Clint and I couldn't finish."

"Oh. Okay." Jake tried to sound indifferent, but Laura could practically see her son salivating as he added, "You can just put it in the fridge and maybe I'll pick at it later."

"Mmm-hmm," Laura replied with a knowing smile while she did what she was told.

She sat down beside her son, and that's when she saw it, lying smack dab in the middle of the table among all the advertisements and the bills: an invitation for Adrian's show.

"Is that...?" Laura's voice trailed off.

"What?" Jake asked as he followed his mother's gaze. "Oh, yeah. That. Yeah, it is," he replied quietly. "Didn't you get yours?"

"I haven't seen anything."

"I told Sam to put you on the list."

"I'm sure she did. I just haven't had time to sort through the mail yet. I'll double-check when I get home. So, that's next weekend already?"

"Yep."

Jake stood up from the table and peered inside the refrigerator with his back to his mother.

Laura bit her lip, but she just couldn't resist. She had to have her suspicions about Jake and Cassie confirmed. "So...are you and Cassie...?"

Jake shot her a dirty look that made her question die on her lips.

"Mom."

"What?" Laura asked defensively.

Jake maintained his evil eye.

"Okay, okay. I'm backing off now."

"Thank you."

I knew it! Laura thought.

"But just remember, I'm always here for you if you need me."

"I know, Mom. I know."

Laura's lips pressed tightly together while the real reason she came to visit her son returned to the forefront of her mind.

This is so not the right time for that.

"Okay, I got to get going," she said as she leaned up on her tiptoes to give him a kiss on his forehead. "Love you."

"Love you too, Mom," Jake replied.

*

Laura thought she might be able to sneak into the house unnoticed, but she wasn't that lucky. Clint nearly scared the hell out of her as he leaned against the archway between the living room and the hallway and asked her how it went.

"It went," she mumbled with a shrug of her shoulders, her eyes diverted away from him.

Clint folded his arms in front of his chest and studied his fiancée's face as if he were a detective interrogating a perp.

"Laura," he said in an accusatory tone.

"What?" she replied as her eyes shot up to meet his.

They stared each other down until Laura couldn't take anymore.

"It just wasn't the right time."

Clint shook his head. "It never is," he muttered under his breath.

Laura's eyes narrowed in anger. "You weren't there," she spat out at him before she stormed upstairs.

Yeah, well, maybe I should've been.

Adrian's eyes widened in horror when she heard the rest of Clint's thoughts.

"Oh, no," she said. "He's not seriously thinking about...?"

"Yes, he is," Kevin answered slowly.

"Oh, this is bad," Adrian said. "So, so bad."

Don't do this, she said as she tried to channel into Clint's thoughts. *Stay out of it. Don't get in the middle of this.*

I already am, Clint responded to his subconscious.

Adrian tilted her head back in defeat while she watched Clint walk out the front door.

"Jake is going to flip," she said.

*

"What are you doing here?" Jake asked when he found Clint at his front door a few minutes later. "If you're looking for my mom, you just missed her."

"Yeah, I know," Clint answered. "I came here to see you. We need to talk."

Jake rolled his eyes. "We have nothing to talk about."

"Yes, we do: your mom."

Jake slowly lowered his arm down away from the door before he walked back inside the apartment. Clint took this as his invitation in.

"You want a beer?" Jake asked as he made his way to the kitchen.

"No, thanks," Clint answered.

Jake took one out of the fridge for himself before he leaned back against the counter.

"So," he said indifferently as he popped the top, "talk."

Clint gripped the chair in front of him. The animosity in the room was stifling, but he was determined to have the conversation with Jake that Laura couldn't.

"She didn't come over today just to bring you food and see how you were doing. She's had something on her mind lately; something she needs to ask you, but she just can't bring herself to do it. So I thought I'd ask for her."

"Ask me what?" Jake replied warily.

Clint cleared his throat. "It's about our wedding."

Every muscle in Jake's body tightened at the mention of his mother getting married. The first thought that came into his mind was the night Adrian died.

That was the night they announced their engagement, and everything blew up after that. I blew up at my mom; Adrian blew up at me; the car....

"Jake?" Clint asked. "You okay?"

"Yeah, I'm fine." He planted his feet firmly on the floor, his back ramrod straight.

"So, your mother would like to know if you would be willing to give her away to me at our wedding."

Kevin scoffed loudly. Adrian looked at him; she couldn't believe her eyes.

He leaned back against the fridge, his arms crossed, teeth bared; his body glowed with an electric green light.

"Hey, Hulk," she teased him, "you need to calm down before you cause a power outage."

Adrian's humor did nothing to lighten Kevin's mood.

Okay, time for plan B. Which is what?

Kevin's thoughts provided her with the answer.

Laura is not yours. She is my wife and she always will be!

Adrian's jaw dropped when she saw Kevin's rage transfer onto Jake.

She is my mother, and there's no way in hell I would ever give her away to you!

"Oh, no! I don't think so," Adrian said defiantly as she came at Kevin with everything she had.

"What the hell is wrong with you?" she shouted as she shoved him as hard as she could. "Can't you see what you're doing to your son?"

It was like she had knocked Kevin back to his senses. His eyes were clearer, and his guilt consumed him once he saw his hatred reflected through Jake.

"Oh, my God," he said, "what have I done?"

"You let your emotions get the best of you," Adrian replied, her voice softer as she began to simmer down. "It happens to the best of us."

Kevin stared at her incredulously. "Who is supposed to be training who here?"

Adrian shrugged. "I think we're both learning from each other, aren't we?"

"Yes, we are," Kevin chuckled. "Now let's see if we can still salvage this somehow."

Kevin stood at the head of the table between both men. Jake still stared daggers at Clint while Clint did his best to ignore it.

"Jake, please," Kevin said as he covered his son's hand with his own, "stop."

"This would mean so much to your mother, Jake," Clint said. "I'm not asking you to do it for me. I'm asking you to do it for her."

Jake's eyes drifted down to his hand. His only thoughts were of his mother.

"I'll think about it," Jake mumbled while his eyes rose up to meet Clint's.

"Thank you."

"Mm-hmm."

"Thank God." Adrian breathed a sigh of relief.

Chapter Twenty-Three

Cassie flipped through the newspaper while she scooped spoonfuls of cereal into her mouth. She nearly choked on her Cheerios when she saw it. The bowl tipped over; milk spilled everywhere, but she didn't care. She was more interested in the headline than anything else. There it was, right on the front page of the arts section: an entire article devoted to Adrian's exhibit this weekend.

Cassie sank into her chair while her lips curved slowly upward into a huge grin.

Damn, if only you could be here to see this.

"Oh, if you only knew," Adrian replied.

This is what we daydreamed about back when we were lying in our beach chairs by the pool. Your first real exhibition!

It was going to be front page news. The paparazzi would be swarming around the red carpet, fighting to get the first exclusive shot of you stepping out of a stylish limo on Jake's arm....

Not me.

Cassie's thoughts shifted back to the night Jake had come over to her apartment for dinner and a movie. He had spotted her invitation on the fridge when he went to get them something to drink.

"What's wrong?" Cassie asked when she caught him staring at it.

"Nothing," Jake answered. "I was just thinking. How would you feel about you and I going to this together?"

The look on Cassie's face said it all.

"That good, huh?"

"No," Cassie replied while she made her way into the kitchen and hopped up on one of the barstools. "It's just that, it's supposed to be Adrian's night. I don't want to do anything to taint it."

"Taint it?" Jake teased her.

"You know what I mean. You know how people are; they'll spend the entire time gossiping about us instead of appreciating Adrian's work."

Jake grunted. "Well, it's up to you. I don't want to make you do anything you're not comfortable with."

But it would mean a lot to me.

"He needs you," Adrian said, stunned that Jake had admitted it to himself.

"He needs you," Adrian said again to Cassie this time. "Don't let him fool you."

All the chaos in Cassie's mind calmed while she looked at Jake, really looked at him. She knew exactly what to do.

Chapter Twenty-Four

"There," Laura said as she turned down the collar of Jake's dress shirt and straightened his tie. "Perfect."

"Thanks, Mom," Jake said. "Got to make sure I look good for tonight."

"You are handsome as always."

"And you," he grinned, "are biased."

"True, but what can I say? You got good genes, kiddo."

Laura grasped her son's trembling hands and stepped back to get a better look at him.

"What?" he asked warily.

"You okay?"

Jake made a face. "Of course," he replied as if the answer were obvious.

"Of course." *Like you'd really tell me if you weren't.* "I'll see you there later, okay."

"Okay."

"And enjoy it," she whispered in his ear as she gave him a hug, "not just for yourself but for Adrian too."

"I will, Mom."

*

Cassie stood in front of the full-length mirror in her bedroom and tried for what felt like the millionth time to clasp her necklace around her neck.

"Goddammit!" she yelled as the chain slipped through her fingers and onto the floor.

"This is a sign." Cassie dropped onto her bed. "It's got to be a sign."

"Yeah," Adrian sat down beside her. "It's a sign you're not meant to wear that necklace tonight."

Her expression turned somber when she saw the panic-stricken look on her best friend's face.

"Oh no," Adrian warned her, "you are not backing out of this now. It's too late. You can't. You're already in your favorite dress and heels. You've got to go."

She turned to Kevin. "She's got to go."

"Only if she wants to," Kevin replied.

Adrian groaned in frustration.

Cassie jumped when she heard a knock at her door.

"And now your ride's here."

Cassie didn't move. The knocking grew louder. Adrian stared at her in disbelief.

"Aren't you going to get that?"

Cassie looked as if she were in a daze, her body paralyzed by fear.

"Cassie? Is everything all right in there?" Jake asked from the other side of the door. "Cass?"

"Don't give in to your fears," Adrian said. "You've got this. All you have to do is answer the door."

He was pounding on the door now. "Cassie!"

"Coming." The word eked out so softly from Cassie's mouth that it was barely audible. She rose to her feet and tried again.

"Coming!" This time he heard her as she made her way down the hall to the front door.

"Good girl," Adrian said while she followed behind her.

Cassie's nerves settled down some once she looked into Jake's eyes.

"Everything okay?" he asked.

"Yeah." *It is now.*

"Good. Now c'mon." Jake pulled her close and kissed the top of her head. "Let's go have some fun."

"Yes, let's," Adrian agreed.

*

They weren't mobbed by the paparazzi outside the gallery. All Cassie could see from the passenger seat of Jake's truck were a few local reporters milling around, which was more than enough for her.

She turned away from the window and caught Jake out of the corner of her eye; he was running his finger around the collar of his navy blue dress shirt as if it were suffocating him. Cassie leaned forward to turn the temperature down.

"Is it just me, or is it roasting in here?" she asked.

"No," he answered with an appreciative smile, "it's not just you."

"Well, thank God! I was afraid I was starting to get hot flashes or something."

They were next in line for valet parking. Jake made sure to open Cassie's door for her. He froze as he was about to hand the keys over to the valet.

Adrian saw fragments of that night flash through Jake's mind: him waiting outside Valentino's for the car, her snatching the keys away from him. The argument they had before they even got into the car.

Oh, hell no! You are not driving anywhere!

Adrian, please. I have to get out of here.

Fine, but I'm driving.

Just drive fast.

Adrian stepped forward to help her husband, but Cassie beat her to it.

She placed her hand around his fist. A small gesture, but it was enough to get Jake to relinquish his keys to the valet.

He squeezed Cassie's hand in gratitude just before a reporter called him over.

The woman seemed nice enough, but Cassie noticed her eyes kept drifting down to their entwined hands.

"Hey!" Adrian snapped at the reporter. "Eyes up front, please. Stay focused on the real story here."

"I don't know about you," Jake said to Cassie after the interview was done, "but I am ready for a drink."

"You read my mind," Cassie replied.

*

They went inside and barely had a chance to steal a glass of champagne from the nearest waiter before Sam swooped in.

"There you are! You had me worried. I'm so glad you made it. Everyone's been asking about you."

And they were off. Sam introduced them to so many people Cassie couldn't possibly remember any of their names if she tried, but she was able to keep track of every sideways glance and disapproving glare cast her way.

And there seemed to be many.

"It's all in your head," Adrian told her, but Cassie wasn't convinced.

Cassie clutched her wrap tighter to her. Jake put his arm around

206 The Last Photograph

Cassie's shoulders; the lady who was speaking to them suddenly lost her train of thought.

Cassie finished her third glass of champagne before she politely excused herself in search of a restroom.

She breathed a sigh of relief once she was safely hidden inside a stall. Her ease was short-lived.

Cassie heard two women come in and start chattering away to each other.

"Oh...my...God!"

"I know, right?"

"Can you believe that?"

"She's practically hanging all over him."

"Takes a lot of nerve, if you ask me, to bring a date to an event honoring your late wife."

Cassie stiffened while her stomach turned.

"Well, you know who she is, don't you?"

"No. Who?"

"The wife's best friend."

"Shut up!"

"I'm serious."

"Wow. Some friend, hey?"

"Can you imagine? I could never."

"Me either. The thought wouldn't even cross my mind."

"That's because you have a conscience."

Cassie shut her eyes tight and folded her arms as if she wanted to shrink inside herself, but Adrian wouldn't let her.

"No! Don't you dare let them run over you like that. They don't even know you! Bunch of big-mouthed bitches! They wouldn't know what a conscience was if it bit them in the ass!"

Kevin gave Adrian a look and let her continue on.

"Don't just sit there! Stand up for yourself and show them who you really are. Don't give them that power over you."

Cassie blamed liquid courage for what she did next. She pushed the stall door open with the palm of her hand and marched toward the women who hovered over the bathroom sinks.

They both turned white as sheets when they saw her.

"Please," Cassie said, "don't stop on my account." They just stared at her with their mouths wide open. "What's the matter? Cat got your tongues? Not so easy to talk about somebody when they're standing right in front of you, is it? Although, I do have to admit, I would have no problem talking about the two of you right now, but I just can't bring myself to sink down to your level."

Adrian grinned from ear-to-ear. "Atta girl! You tell them!"

"Well," Cassie continued as she tossed her paper towel in the garbage, "I've said my piece. I'll leave the two of you alone now so you can finish the rest of your conversation."

Cassie shook like a leaf and her heart pounded in her chest as she hurried down the hallway, but that was nothing compared to how she felt when she rounded the corner and saw Jake.

Chapter Twenty-Five

He looked as if he were staring at a ghost. Cassie rushed over to him. "Jake, what's wrong?" she asked.

He didn't answer; he didn't need to.

Cassie followed his heartbroken eyes to the enlarged photograph that took up most of the wall before them.

It was a close-up of Jake. He lay in bed, his right arm flung out across the pillow; his head nestled on his arm, and his long blonde bangs fell haphazardly into his eyes. The caption below it read: *The Last Photograph: July 21, 2015.*

Cassie was no expert in photography, but she did know that picture moved her.

"Oh, Jake," she whispered.

"I knew what Sam was planning, but still," Adrian said, "to see it up close and personal like this."

"Imagine how Jake felt," Kevin replied. "He wasn't prepared for this at all."

Jake's chest tightened; he shut his eyes while moments from that morning played out like a never-ending slideshow through his mind:

How she had yelled at him after he had ruined her shot once again; the angry face she couldn't maintain once he got close enough to her; how gorgeous she looked lying underneath him, and again moments later above him before they made love; the high-pitched squeal she let out when he carried her into their shower.

Never again, Jake thought. *Never again.*

Adrian took a step toward him, but Kevin stopped her.

"I got this," he told her.

He strode over to his son and grasped both of his shoulders. Their eyes locked; Kevin nodded firmly.

Jake fought to uphold his Riley stance after his father released him, even while the tears poured out of him.

Cassie threw her arms around Jake, not giving a damn about what anyone thought or said. Her only concern at that moment was him.

"It's all right," she whispered to Jake as she cradled the back of his head in her hand and pulled him closer to her. His arms eventually curled around her; his face hidden in the crook of her neck.

"It's all right," Cassie said again as she cried with him.

She wiped her eyes and saw Laura making her way to them, pushing away as many cell phones in the process as she could. She stopped short once she cleared the crowd. Cassie gave her a reassuring smile.

"C'mon," Cassie gently urged Jake. "Your mom's waiting."

Jake rose up, strong as ever, and took Cassie's hand in his. His mother wrapped her arm around his waist and guided them to the nearest exit. It didn't take long for Sam to intercept them.

She looked worse than Jake did.

"Oh, my God, Jake!" Sam apologized profusely after she pulled him aside so they could speak in private. "I am so sorry! I never would've included that photograph if I knew it was going to upset you so much."

"It's all right," Jake told her. *I didn't know either.*

*

Laura stood outside talking on her phone to one of her brothers when she saw Jake leaving the gallery.

"Bobby, I got to go. Just make sure the pizzeria's cleared out by the time we get there okay. We'll see you in a little bit. Bye."

She tossed her cell phone into her handbag and hurried over to her son.

"Hey, you know you've got nothing to be ashamed of, right?"

"Yeah, I know."

"I'm serious." She grabbed his chin and forced him to look her in the eye. "Your dad would understand."

"I know," Jake responded adamantly. *Believe me, I know. I felt it.*

Adrian's eyes darted wildly over to Kevin.

"So that whole shoulder-grabbing thing you did to him?" she asked.

"He got the gist with that, yeah," Kevin replied nonchalantly, "but he'll never admit it out loud to anyone."

"Well, of course not," Adrian said sarcastically. "That is the Riley way."

Adrian shook her head in disbelief. "And you say women are hard to figure out."

*

Laura's brothers pulled it off; Mama Jo's was empty except for Cassie and Jake who sat across from each other in awkward silence.

"C'mon," Adrian pleaded from her seat beside Cassie. "Somebody say something, please."

I can't, Cassie thought. *Everything I'm coming up with just sounds so…stupid.*

"And you?" Adrian asked her husband. "What's your excuse?"

It's too quiet, Jake thought.

"Well, do something about it!"

"Hey, Cass," he said, dead serious, "would you mind doing something for me?"

"Yeah, sure. Whatever you need."

"Go play some music, please. I know my mom meant well, but this place feels like a damn morgue now."

Cassie laughed as she took the money from his outstretched hand. "Any requests?"

"Anything upbeat."

"You got it."

"Thank you." Jake slid out of the booth and planted a quick kiss on her lips. "I'm going to grab another beer. You want one?"

"Yes, please."

"I'll be right back."

Jake headed up to the bar, then stopped mid-stride when he caught sight of what was happening in the kitchen. He pulled up the nearest stool and sat back to watch Laura in full-on Mom mode.

She moved swiftly around the kitchen in her high heels as if they were Nike track shoes. Yeast and pizza sauce stained the black apron she had tied over her new red dress. Strands of her dark hair fell loosely around her face as she peeked inside the brick oven. A soft smile of satisfaction rose to her lips while she brought the pizza toward her.

Ahhh...perfection! Laura thought.

"Wow," Adrian sighed while she propped her chin up with the palm of her hand, "she is amazing."

"Yes, she is," Kevin agreed.

"How does she do it?"

"She's a mom, and moms will do anything for their children," Kevin answered.

Adrian looked over at her husband. "I think Jake might be starting to realize that now too."

Here she is making homemade pizza for me, happy as a clam, and I'm sitting here feeling sorry for myself.

"Jake...honey...are you all right?" Laura asked as she approached the bar.

"Yeah. Yeah, I'm fine. You've...uh...you've got some flour in your hair or something," Jake motioned toward her bangs.

"Oh, thanks. Guess I got a little carried away back there," she said as she quickly brushed it away. "So, the breadsticks are all done; I'm just waiting for the pizza to cool off and we should be all set."

Jake stared at her incredulously. *Breadsticks too?*

"Mom, you know you didn't have to do all of that."

"All of what? It was nothing," Laura replied with a shrug of her shoulders. "You were hungry; I made you food. It's no big deal."

Yeah, it is, Jake thought. *You've always done so much for me; now maybe it's time I do something for you.*

"I'll do it," he told her.

"Do what?" she asked bewildered.

"Give you away..." he paused to swallow the lump of pride that formed in his throat, "to Clint."

Laura's eyes nearly popped out of her head.

"I must be hallucinating," she said as she dropped down onto the stool beside her, "because I could've swore I just heard you say—"

"I'll give you away to Clint."

Laura still couldn't believe it. "But how did you? I mean, I never even asked...."

And then it came to her. *Clint.*

"He talked to you, didn't he?" she asked.

"Yes, Clint talked to me, but he did not talk me into anything."

"Oh, I have no doubt about that." *That's why I'm going to do this.*

"Mom, what are you doing?" Jake asked nervously when he saw Laura coming around the counter to him.

"Thanking you," she said.

Jake braced himself for his mother's emotional embrace. Adrian sighed in exasperation while she watched her husband's body instinctively stiffen into its rigid Riley stance while he willed every tear away.

"What?" Kevin teased her. "You didn't really think we could get rid of it that easily, did you?"

"A girl can dream, can't she?"

Chapter Twenty-Six

The heat drained Jake the second he stepped out of his air-conditioned truck, which did nothing to improve his mood.

He rolled his head and flexed his arms as if he were a fighter just before a title match.

Christ, Jake thought. *I feel like I'm trapped inside a straightjacket or something.*

Adrian looked to Kevin. "Have all the Riley men always been such crab asses about dressing up?"

"Mmmm...pretty much...yeah."

Jake grumbled and groaned until he reached the foot of the stairs inside his mother's house.

"Mom," he hollered, "where are you? Are you ready to go?"

"I'm in my bedroom, Jake," she shouted down to him. "Just give me five more minutes."

"Five more minutes," he muttered sarcastically under his breath. "Yeah, right."

Laura stared out her bedroom window, mesmerized by the sickly yellow haze that hung over the sky.

Something's coming, she thought while she absently twirled her necklace between her fingers.

"You know," Adrian said from across the room, "I've heard rain on your wedding day is a sign of good luck."

"I don't think she's worried about the weather," Kevin replied.

Laura's eyes drifted away from the sky and down to her first wedding ring.

I haven't taken this off since the day you gave it to me twenty-seven years ago. I never even considered it until today.

"You can," Kevin responded as he stood behind his wife. "I'm okay with it if you are."

Laura's hands reached back and met Kevin's. She swore she caught a whiff of his cologne as they slowly unclasped the necklace together. It slid gently into the palm of her hand just as Jake knocked on the door.

"Mom, I hope you're decent," he said while he swung the door open, "because I'm coming in."

"Whoa." Jake forgot whatever else he was about to say when he saw his mother standing in front of the mirror in her wedding dress.

It was a sleeveless, full-length satin gown with a plunging neckline that was partially hidden by a patch of lace across the chest. Her long, dark hair—which Jake had only ever seen either hanging straight down or in a ponytail—was pulled back into loose, curly ringlets. She wore a subtle shade of red lipstick and lined her eyes just enough to transform her from pretty to drop-dead gorgeous. And, last but not least, were the teardrop diamond earrings that adorned her ears.

"What's wrong?" she asked when she saw the stunned expression on her son's face.

"Nothing," Jake answered as he shook his head in disbelief. "Just... whoa."

"I agree," Kevin said as he kissed her on the nape of her neck. "Makes me wish I were the groom-to-be all over again."

Laura blushed while the skin on her neck and arms turned to gooseflesh.

"Aw, thank you, honey," she told Jake.

Her look was complete, except for one thing Jake couldn't help but notice was missing.

"Where is it?" he asked curiously.

Laura's free hand instantly shot up to her neck. Her eyes drifted ruefully down to her clenched fist. Her fingers slowly uncurled to reveal her wedding ring from Kevin.

Jake approached his mother tentatively, as if she were holding an ancient treasure. They stared reverently at the plain, gold band for the longest time.

"I've thought long and hard about this, Jacob," Laura began.

"You don't need to explain," Jake replied.

"Yes, I do. This ring," she picked it up and held it between her finger and thumb, "is a symbol of how much your father and I loved each other. And you are a direct result of that love, which is why I can't think of anyone better to take care of it for me."

Take care of it for me.

Those words brought Jake back to the end of every conversation he had ever had with his dad before Kevin headed back out on the road.

"Now remember," Kevin would tell him, "you're the man of the family while I'm gone. So I'm counting on you to take care of your mom for me."

"Yes, sir," Jake would respond.

He was counting on me, Jake thought now. *That's what I always*

thought about every time some guy would hit on her or take her out on a
date after he died. It was up to me to take care of her for him.

"I had no idea," Kevin said.

"Oh, c'mon," Adrian replied. "What do you mean, you had no idea? Aren't you supposed to know everything?"

"Not about that, I didn't. This is the first time Jake's ever thought about it around me."

"Oh. Well," Adrian said, "you must've left a pretty strong impression because it's stuck with him all this time."

I did a pretty good job of it, too, Jake continued. *I kept every asshole and idiot away from her. None of them ever wanted to deal with the baggage of a kid, much less one that raised as much hell as I did.*

Until Clint came along.

Nothing I did could scare him off, so after a while, I started to feel like I had let my dad down.

Jake's shoulders sagged from the weight of the nagging guilt as Laura pressed the ring into his hand.

"What's wrong?" she asked.

"Nothing," Jake mumbled. "I was just thinking about Dad."

Laura groaned in frustration.

"Come here," she said as she motioned toward the mirror.

Jake did as he was told. They stood together, mother and son, and faced their reflections.

"You want to know what a real man is? All you have to do is look in the mirror. And I have no doubt that your father would feel exactly the same way."

"She's right," Kevin said as he stood on the other side of his son.

"Thanks, Mom," Jake replied while he rose up to his full height.

Laura stepped up on her tiptoes to kiss him and left a faint red impression on his forehead.

"C'mon," she smiled. "You don't want to make me late for my own wedding now, do you?"

*

Jake stood in the back of the church, his mother's arm looped through his. Their eyes were fixated on the altar before them while bittersweet memories from their past took hold of their hearts.

Laura gave her son's arm a supportive squeeze as the organist began to play "The Wedding March."

"It's time for us to move forward," she told him.

They exchanged knowing smiles.

"I'm ready whenever you are," Jake replied.

They began their slow procession down the aisle with Kevin by his wife's side, and when the priest asked, "Who gives this woman away?" Jake and his father said in unison, "I do."

Clint and Jake nodded respectfully to each other after Jake placed his mother's hand in Clint's.

Kevin pulled slowly away from his wife, his eyes closed so he could remember the touch of her hand as it slipped through his fingers.

Laura's heart suddenly felt at peace while she stepped up to the altar with Clint. She glanced up at the ceiling with a grateful smile.

Thank you, sweetheart.

Kevin bowed his head humbly. "I just want you to be happy."

Meanwhile, Jake took his seat in the front pew beside Cassie and slipped his arm lovingly around her shoulders.

"I'm impressed," Kevin said to Adrian while she calmly watched them from the altar. "You finally tamed the green-eyed monster."

"I just want him to be happy," Adrian replied sincerely.

"Good. That means you're ready."

"Ready for what?"

"This."

Adrian followed Kevin's lead; their eyes drawn to the entrance of the church, which was suddenly bathed in magnificent colors.

"Oh, my God. I've seen this before, haven't I?"

"Yes, you have," Kevin answered. "Those are your lights; they're welcoming you home."

Adrian moved toward them, then stopped once she realized Kevin wasn't with her.

"Aren't you coming?"

"I wish I could, but I can't. This is one journey you have to take on your own."

Adrian's face fell.

"Don't worry. I'll be here waiting for you when you come back."

"I'm coming back?"

"Well, yeah. I'm good, but there's no way I can watch over these two by myself."

"So I get to stay with Jake permanently?" Adrian asked hopefully.

"That's something you'll have to discuss with Him," Kevin answered, "along with a few other things. But I wouldn't take too long. He hates to be kept waiting."

Adrian didn't need to be told twice. She proceeded without hesitation and delved into the breathtaking light just as a loud clap of thunder roared through the sky.

Jake tuned out the ceremony for a moment while he listened intently to the song he believed the storm was playing just for him.

About the Author

Anne Miller is the youngest of four children. She was born in West Allis, Wisconsin and moved with her family to the Upper Peninsula of Michigan when she was two years old. Her passion for writing began when she was ten years old when she wrote her first novel, *The Summer Murder*, and she hasn't quit since.

She attended the University of Wisconsin-Green Bay for two-and-a-half years where she majored in English-Creative Writing with a minor in Communications.

After college, Anne excelled at several different day jobs throughout the years, including grocery store clerk, hotel night auditor, and hospital housekeeper. She is currently a customer service representative/bank teller at a local financial institution. All of her job positions have enhanced her storytelling skills.

Anne is also a die-hard Green Bay Packers fan. She enjoys reading, and her latest obsession is the Outlander series of novels. She lives in the same small town she grew up in and shares a home with her sister. *The Last Photograph* is her first published novel.

You can visit Anne at her website:

www.millerslastphotograph.com

Made in the USA
Columbia, SC
21 October 2017